Paul Andrews

Stop Mark Robins

Austin Macauley
Publishers Ltd.

A CIP catalogue record for this title is available from the British Library.

ISBN 9781786125422 (Paperback)
ISBN 9781786125439 (Hardback)
ISBN 9781786125446 (E-Book)

www.austinmacauley.com

First Published (2016)
Austin Macauley Publishers Ltd.
25 Canada Square
Canary Wharf
London
E14 5LQ

Prologue

Sunday 7th January 1990 saw a goal scored by Mark Robins that was arguably the most important in English league football history; as it ensured that Sir Alex Ferguson would go on to provide a magnificent trophy laden legacy for Manchester United. It was a legacy that would see Manchester United eventually overtake Liverpool in league titles, as well as adding 2 Champions League titles to their collection including that mesmeric triumph against Bayern Munich in 1999, where 2 sensational late goals overturned what looked like probably defeat.

Sir Alex Ferguson was a wonderful manger that gave Manchester United wonderful times, but in 1990 he had been in the Manchester United hot seat for 4 years & there had been no trophies to show for it & there was increasing speculation that his job might be on the line if Manchester United didn't win a trophy soon. The F A cup tie at Nottingham Forest was a difficult one, but it was one that Manchester United dared not lose or the pressure could have proved too great for Manchester United. The F A cup represented Manchester United greatest chance to win a trophy as they weren't in the running to win the league, this would be won by the mighty red machine Liverpool whom had enjoyed an incredible era of golden dominance in the English game, but incredibly this would be the last time Liverpool would win the title right up to the present day.

It was unthinkable at that point in time that Liverpool's amount of titles wins would ever be surpassed & certainly it didn't look like it would be by Manchester United as at that time they hadn't won a title for 23 years, but thanks to Mark Robins scoring a winning goal for Manchester United at Nottingham Forest a very tricky hurdle had been cleared & Manchester United duly went on to win the F A cup that year, providing Sir Alex Ferguson the breathing space to set in place his magnificent legacy of incredible success but what if Mark Robins never scored that goal? What might have happened then to provide such a different future?

Josh Stanton an avid Liverpool fan found himself stuck in the year 1989(accidently & unable to resist the urge to tamper with football history was about to find out you mess with time at your peril, what was he going to discover?

Chapter 1

May 2010

To all intents and purposes Josh Stanton was your typical Liverpool teenager, born on 10th April 1993, just turned 17, Josh was full of the confident exuberance of youth, friends were plentiful and life was fun. Like most lads he was totally into football and on Merseyside you were either a "Red" or a "Blue" (Liverpool or Everton). Josh Stanton was very much a Liverpool fan, in fact a massive fan with an encyclopaedic knowledge of everything to do with Liverpool FC. There was nothing he didn't know about them, such was his love for them. Josh Stanton modelled his thirst for knowledge on his favourite defender and Liverpool legend, Jamie Carragher, who was renowned for his own encyclopaedic knowledge of football. Josh Stanton was very much football mad.

Merseyside could be a very special place to live as rivalry between Liverpool and Everton was generally incredibly friendly compared to other cities and areas. It could be so special that a whole multitude of families could contain both Liverpool and Everton fans in the same family; there was an incredible tolerance of each other on Merseyside, a mutual respect between both sets of fans. Indeed, Josh Stanton's best friend was Ryan Brown, a staunch Evertonian. They enjoyed lots of friendly banter displayed with typical scouse wit and humour; their verbal jousts were something to behold and Josh Stanton usually gained the upper hand thanks to, in a small part, Liverpool being an extremely successful football club, a club that had won 18 League Titles and 5 European Cups in their glorious history. Liverpool were regarded as the most successful football club in English football, so Josh could often win his friendly arguments with Ryan Brown and his Evertonian friends, but Everton were also a great club in their own right and could boast a glorious history. They were known as "The People's Club" and could still pack a punch, so Josh Stanton never had it totally his own way in their banter, but it was all good.

Liverpool was a special place for another reason and that was the proximity of their grounds to each other. All that separated Liverpool FC Anfield Stadium and Everton FC Goodison Park was Stanley Park, a very welcome oasis of green that provided a beautiful breathing space between these two great clubs and provided a welcome haven in its football pitches where Josh Stanton and Ryan Brown, together with their mates, would often have their very own versions of the Merseyside derby, often played out there to equal passion and fervour that would be experienced in the real thing. No quarter was asked or given in these games and could get very spicy indeed but afterwards there was a very real friendship and respect. That's how it should be! That's how it was! Josh Stanton was a very popular young man on Merseyside and he was loving life, he didn't realise what was literally going to be around the corner but he soon would.

Fig 1a Stanley Park
(South looking towards Liverpool FC
Anfield is central just peeping over trees)

After each game played in Stanley Park, Josh would always make a point of saluting the south side of the park, this was where Liverpool FC resided on Anfield Road. Josh's heart and soul lay with the reds and he would often gaze lovingly in their direction, but laying just behind Liverpool's main stand was an area of derelict houses, all or most boarded up, to be very honest it was not the best sight to look at and it was especially unflattering being so close to the football Mecca that was Anfield stadium. But in these derelict houses, one was going to house a truly astonishing sight behind its neglected exterior, something that would transport Josh into one extraordinary adventure after another and lead him to a temptation he just couldn't resist, something that would tear at the very fabric of time and football history and that would be to stop Mark Robins. Stop him cementing the opportunity for the best manager ever in the British game arguably to establish himself at Manchester United, when allegedly he was under a very real threat of the sack. Mark Robins was portrayed by many people as the man that saved Sir Alex Ferguson by scoring arguably the most important goal in English football history at Nottingham Forest in January 1990 and Josh was somehow deliberately going to sabotage this. How was he going to do it? What repercussions would be reaped if Josh did change football history?

For Josh Stanton, sabotaging Manchester United was personal, of he ever got the chance! As it just happened that it was a callous maniacal driver who was responsible for the tragic death of his beloved and greatly missed father, Peter Stanton. The driver that caused the accident through driving in a reckless, irresponsible manner turned out to be a Manchester United fan and to make it worse, he showed absolutely no remorse for his actions, the man showed zero respect. All this was in December 1998, when Josh was just a delightfully cute 5 year old boy, excitingly looking forward to seeing his dad come home from work and play with him, like doting dads do, poor Mr Peter Stanton never made it home. Josh and his dad's special relationship had been taken tragically away and Josh had to work hard ever so hard to hide his permanent heartache.

Josh Stanton would never get to experience the magic of his Liverpool-supporting dad taking him, all awestruck and starry eyed, into the magical arena of Anfield and into the famous Kop end. Josh would never experience with his dad the sheer elation and drama of a big football match played out in front of such a frenzied partisan crowd generating a soaring choral atmosphere, Josh was never going to experience with his dad the sheer goose pimple effect of singing Liverpool's famous anthem "You'll Never Walk Alone" which would literally make the hairs on your neck stand up, poor Josh was being deprived of the joy may sons got to experience with their dads, many millions of sons! What made a bad situation so much worse was the fact that the driver responsible for his dad's death got a totally derisory sentence and even showed remarkable glee in what he had done as Mr Stanton was a Liverpool fan. The man was warped! The man had no shame! There had been very little justice applied here and Josh Stanton was the sort of determined young lad that would not rest until it happened.

The whole disliking for this man's team, Manchester United, was going to be made worse and made unbearable in terms of wanting justice or karma during the next year, in 1999, as Manchester United achieved a magnificent treble, including the never to be forgotten Champions League trophy in an amazing climax to the final in Barcelona's Nou Camp Stadium, as Manchester United came from behind to beat Bayern Munich 2-1. This was excruciatingly difficult for Josh to see what was now a great nemesis doing so well and seeing their wild celebrations was certainly not justice in Josh Stanton's heart, this most certainly was not fair, it was not justice at all! Sir Alex Ferguson was proving to be a truly brilliant manager, so much so that there was a real danger that Manchester United could override Liverpool as the most successful club in England. Josh Stanton would never ever want this to happen and even more importantly neither would his dad; Manchester United had to be stopped by any means possible.

Having turned 17, Josh Stanton had showed outstanding academic strengths in science and astrophysics and had been awarded a special place at Manchester College as a result under the tutorship of Mr Xavier Richardson, a brilliantly engrossing man with fascinating theories on time travel. He was riveting to listen to and a genuinely nice man as well. Josh Stanton had maximised his potential as a tribute to his dad, he was turning into a fine young man and Josh knew he wanted his dad to be proud of him so he was very motivated. Josh Stanton was doing so well that that his times with Ryan Brown, his best friend, were getting less so. They were anxious to enjoy their increasingly precious times when they did get together and none more so than on the pitches of Stanley Park.

Josh's heart and soul may have laid with the south side of the park but when heading for home it was with Ryan Brown in an opposite northwards direction from Stanley Park; they were heading for Goodison Park and beyond. Ryan Brown, and unbelievably a reluctant Josh Stanton too, lived in a street that was right behind Everton FC Goodison Park. Josh Stanton lived in Gwlady's Street right behind the fiercely vocal Gwlady's Street end of Goodison Park – it was directly behind Everton's partisan kop! Oh, the irony of it all! Josh Stanton, a super reds nut, was a Gwladys Street resident. Josh Stanton's bedroom faced directly onto Liverpool FC's local rivals. His bedroom was a massive, a whole shrine to everything Liverpool FC and contained a whole plethora of memorabilia, including massive posters of Steven Gerrard and the mighty reds lifting the Champions League trophy in 2005 (the miracle where they came from 0-3 down at half-time to win on penalties) this was a truly wondrous game, but it made Josh very sad at the same time as all he could think of was his beloved dad missing out on such a historical game, it might have been Liverpool's finest hour and his dad wasn't there to enjoy it with him. His dad would've gone crazy with happiness but it wasn't meant to be!

It was coming up to the end of June 2010 and life at Manchester College was getting very intriguing for Josh as he had begun to notice the new English Literature tutor, in fact Josh could not take his eyes off her and very weirdly it seemed she could not take her eyes off him. It was extremely odd as Josh was only 17 and this lady tutor was a good twenty years older. Josh was unsettled at how he was beginning to feel there was a strong gut feeling that there was something very special about her. The lady tutor was Emma Chambers, a Miss Emma Chambers and she seemed so full of mystery. Why did Josh have such a weird feeling about her and why was it being reciprocated? Josh had never experienced such feelings before as he felt like he had met her before and yet he hadn't, but he couldn't explain why he had such a strong feeling of deja vu and this lady was absolutely enchanting. Josh could feel his heart race when he looked at her and then could notice it being returned with interest. There was an overwhelming feeling that somehow they were extremely close but how on earth could that be? It seemed like she knew something, something she wanted to share with Josh. It was all very weird. Josh was glad term would soon be over as this Emma Chambers was beginning to dominate his every thought.

Josh Stanton was very glad to have the welcome company of Ryan Brown to look forward to as a way of distracting his troublesome thoughts but as he and Ryan ventured out towards Stanley Park, Josh Stanton was going to be provided with the ultimate rollercoaster ride of his life. Josh Stanton was going to go forward to the past and be back to the future, his life was never going to be the same again! Just what was waiting for him?

Chapter 2

The Last House on The Street

July 1st 2010

It was a beautiful sunny day in the city of Liverpool but Josh Stanton was bored, very bored! The football season was over, no adrenaline rush to go see his beloved Liverpool FC or verbal jousting with his Everton friends to look forward to until August arrived, summer was just a barren desert for this football junkie. Maybe it was a blessing as Liverpool FC in the year 2010 had become a bit ordinary and accumulated some substantial debt under unpopular American owners with no trophies won last year, and an unsightly seventh place finish going with that. The stench of staleness was getting depressingly greater. Ooh, how that magical, glorious night in Istanbul 2005, when Liverpool won the Champions League in the most magnificent comeback, was becoming more distant with each passing year. Ooh, how that was the greatest night of Josh Stanton's life, but in other ways the saddest, as it brought home how much his dad would have loved that and he wasn't around to witness it.

Josh Stanton, this fine summer's day, was walking near his beloved Anfield. He and Ryan Brown, just by chance that day, decided to detour the streets behind Liverpool main stand which was peculiar as this area of streets, in places, was particularly shabby, with lots of dated houses lying vacant and boarded up – all lifeless and depressing. This wasn't a place to be proud of even though it was close to the magical area of Liverpool FC Anfield Stadium.

Ryan Brown was dismissively unimpressed and not going to hang around in "such a dump" and urged Josh Stanton to come to Stanley Park and have some fun. Josh Stanton reluctantly agreed and they were about to leave this area when Josh Stanton's gaze was distracted by a strange blue glow coming from behind the last house in the street, one of the many that was boarded up, but nevertheless it had a strange glow emanating from inside. Josh wanted to explore further and Ryan reluctantly agreed to check it out with him. Together they dismantled some of the boards fronting the main window and climbed through. What was this strange glow? It was coming from a spherical shape that filled half the hallway, a bit like a giant bubble. Ryan was freaked out and was going to report it but Josh wanted to find out more.

"Don't step inside it!" yelled Ryan. Josh was dismissive.

"What's to worry about, Ryan, it's just a big bubble." Josh proceeded to edge nearer.

"Come on, Josh, let's go! You don't know what it is," urged Ryan. An ever more agitated Josh just shrugged his shoulders and said, "Nothing ventured, nothing gained!" and entered the bubble.

For what must have been something like only a few seconds, half a minute at the most, Josh just stood nonplussed inside this bubble. There was nothing to write home about, it was no big deal. "Ryan, come in, it's harmless." There was no reply "Ryan, come in you ignorant git!" Josh yelled. Still no reply. Josh Stanton stepped out. There was no Ryan Brown standing there, where had he gone? "Ryan, come back you chicken," laughed Josh. It was soon to be no laughing matter; Ryan Brown was nowhere to be seen anywhere, where was he? Surely he couldn't be too far away?

Josh Stanton left the boarded house and straight away things seemed a little different – there seemed to be less houses boarded up for a start. Still no sign of Ryan so Josh decided to go home, crossing Stanley Park. A glance back towards Anfield Road and the outline of Liverpool's ground seemed a little different. Josh rubbed his eyes; must drink less, was his overriding thought, but as he cut through the lake area of Stanley Park the sight of Goodison Park cut a sobering reality stake through his heart. It was different, the park stand was most definitely different! What the hell was happening here? 'This can't be real,' Josh thought. 'Am I dreaming?'

Josh headed for the other side of Everton's ground to Gwladys Street, where he lived. His front door was no longer black, but green! This was unreal! Josh tried his front door key to let himself in but it wouldn't turn the lock so he knocked on the door and Josh was just about to be frozen with shock! It was his mother that came to the front door, but she was younger! Much younger! Josh Stanton's mother was 40 years old but staring him in the face was someone just out of her teenage years.

"What do you want?" she asked. Josh just stood there open mouthed in utter disbelief. "If you're a double glazing canvasser I'm not interested," she said promptly and shut the door.

"Oh my god, this can't be happening to me!" Josh wailed. "What do I do now, where do I go?" The first thing Josh decided to do was go to the local newsagents and there, staring him in the face, was the date: Friday 1st September 1989. This starkly confirmed Josh Stanton's worst nightmare: somehow he was in the past. "It must have been that strange bubble in that boarded house," Josh mused so off he went to return to that boarded up house and to his horror there was no longer a strange emanating glow coming from this place; no bubble! "Oh hell, I am in deep trouble now. I need to think what to do! Nobody knows me in 1989; I'm not supposed to exist! My own mum just totally blanked me!"

Josh Stanton's nightmare was true reality.

Chapter 3

It's Not So Bad

24 hours had elapsed; Josh Stanton had experienced a very uncomfortable night sleeping rough in Stanley Park, but it was time to try and crystallise his thoughts, clear his head and come to terms with this unbelievable situation that he was in. Josh Stanton needed to plan a way ahead in getting somewhere to stay and getting some money to pay for it. A massive brainwave suddenly emerged into Josh Stanton's head.

"If this is 1989, I know through my fervent knowledge of Liverpool's history how they will get on in their football matches; I'll be able to milk the bookies, money won't be a problem," sighed a massively relieved Josh. Then another brainwave hit him like a thunderbolt. "1989-1990 season... Liverpool win the league this season, I've never seen Liverpool win a league championship; my dad had – oh my god, my dad! If this is 1989 my dad is still alive!" Josh Stanton suddenly was a quivering wreck of overwhelming emotion, how would he react to seeing his dad for the first time since he was little? What would his dad be like in the past?

Would they get on and would Josh dare tell his dad who he was and what was going to happen in the future? Questions, questions! And not only that, Josh had to work out what had happened to him and how to resolve it. Did Josh Stanton want it resolving? All of a sudden being in 1989 wasn't so bad.

First thing's first, Josh Stanton needed to make money and get a list of Liverpool fixtures to see if he could remember how they got on and see if there was anything else he could remember about this year where he could capitalise on his knowledge. Maybe he could befriend dad by sharing his knowledge or winnings. It seemed a good start and an innocent way of getting to know him, Josh looked at the paper to see who Liverpool were playing that Saturday. Derby County away. Josh wasn't totally sure if Liverpool won that game but he was prepared to gamble that they did and proceeded to put all his money, all £50, on them doing so. Josh Stanton stood to make a healthy profit if they did and he would gain time to breathe a bit easier, but should Liverpool fail, Josh was penniless and in big trouble! It was a massive gamble but Josh needed to make money and make it fast!

Josh Stanton was as nervous as he ever was that Saturday afternoon (September 2nd 1989). Stakes were very high indeed; there was no Sky Sports News like he was used to, so Josh had to rely on passers-by and nosing through the local electrical store's shop window at their display of televisions.

The gamble was about to pay off, as Liverpool won comfortably – Derby County 0, Liverpool 3, phew! Breathing space gained, money doubled, Josh Stanton could now start to plan things. Step one –try and get a roof over his head and get a meal down inside him, then look to see who Liverpool played next week and work out if he knew what would happen and how much he could profit from it.

Josh Stanton couldn't believe his luck when he looked to check who Liverpool were playing next, Crystal Palace at home! Josh Stanton knew with 100% certainty what happened and it was an extraordinary result which was probably why Josh could remember it. Josh was ecstatic! He knew Liverpool were going to win 9-0; what were the odds on that! Josh knew that winnings of betting on 9-0 would net him thousands! And that would be from only putting a fraction of his money, leaving him to be able to buy a ticket to go and see the match and watch Anfield legends like Ian Rush, John Barnes, and Peter Beardsley in real-life action. Josh Stanton knew Liverpool were going to win 9-0 and he so wanted to be able to watch this game, or any game for that matter, with his dad – something cruelly deprived to him by a callous United fan in 1998 when Josh was just 5 1/2 years old. Josh Stanton had a week to get to know his dad, but apart from that, Josh could relax knowing his money troubles were going to be over soon.

Josh Stanton had a vague memory of his dad liking to taking him to a family pub when he was little and knew his dad was proud of his pool prowess, so Josh thought of a cunning plan to get himself a foothold into his dad's life; he just hoped his dad would visit this pub so he could put this plan into action. True to form his dad would appear and Josh could seize his chance if his composure didn't fail. This was a truly momentous moment; a chance to see his dad for the first time since he was a little boy. He possessed various photos of his dad in his prime, indeed a most poignant one of his dad kicking a football around in the garden with a 5 year old Josh it took pride of place within Josh's wallet. How emotional is this going to be? Josh so loved his dad and missed him so much and now was going to see him, albeit as a slim, toned, 22 year old man which was only 5 years older than Josh was. They could be best buddies, how very weird!

It was 9.30pm, Josh had been at the club for half an hour when the momentous moment materialised. The pub door opened and in walked Peter Stanton with a couple of mates and after getting their drinks, they duly proceeded to the pool table. It was operating a winner-stays-on policy and they duly put their money on the table knowing how good his dad was at pool with winning and staying on. There was a very good chance he would get to play his dad and be able to implement his plan to get to know him better. In the meantime Josh couldn't take his eyes off his dad; this was so surreal! If he didn't watch himself he would get a thumping as Peter Stanton wouldn't appreciate being eyed up so intensely, but Josh was in a state of utter fascination and awe. As predicted, Peter Stanton was beating everybody at the pool table, it was now Josh's turn to play him. Josh was so nervous he could hardly breathe and his cue was shaking violently. It was Josh's break. Embarrassingly, Josh produced an air shot. Everybody burst out laughing, but this would be a welcome ice breaker to Josh and gave him the courage to raise the stakes, suggesting that the loser has to pay for the winner to go to the Liverpool v Crystal Palace match at the weekend knowing full well that's what he wanted. Peter Stanton duly 7-balled Josh, but seemed enchanted by his young rival and agreed to have a ticket paid for by Josh. Job done! Josh's plan had worked!

"By the way, what do you do for a living?" asked a quizzical Peter.

"Professional Gambler," came an instant reply.

"What made you go down that line?" asked an even more quizzical Peter. Josh had to think for a minute as he knew he couldn't dare admit he was from the future as Peter would think he was crazy and want nothing to do with him.

"I'm psychic; I possess psychic abilities." Peter was very sceptical.

"Yeah, right!" he sarcastically replied. "See you on Saturday." Josh nodded.

"Yes I'll see you then, meet me by the Shankly Gates." Josh was made up, Saturday couldn't come quick enough, though Josh couldn't resist adding, "You won't want to miss this match, I can feel a goal glut happening!"

Josh was so happy and full of joy, all he could think of was Saturday and watching Liverpool legends at his beloved Anfield with his beloved dad, albeit strictly on a mate basis. Friday afternoon at the bookies was pure theatre as the cashier took £30 from Josh for Liverpool to win 9-0 at odds of 500-1. "You're totally crazy, don't you like money?" She exclaimed.

"See you on Monday for my winnings," came a cocky reply. Josh was just so full of it. Saturday had come around and Josh waited nervously for Peter to arrive. He hoped his plan had worked and lo and behold it had.

"Come on then, Kop End, here we come!" This was the moment Josh's heart had yearned for, walking round towards the Kop. It was weird seeing Anfield without the Centenary Stand's towering presence from Kemlyn Road, then an even more weird overpowering feeling would embrace Josh once he entered the Kop – it was still in its magical terrace era! Josh was just awestruck at the majesty of it all, the atmosphere felt so much more vibrant and intense compared to what Josh was used to in his time, he could feel the goose pimples as the pre-match signature tune "You'll Never Walk Alone" was played for the heaving masses on the Kop to belt out with feverous gusto. This was just heavenly for Josh as he and his dad joined in with all the intense euphoric enthusiasm and emotion. All they could muster never was "You'll Never Walk Alone". It was so blissfully poignant.

The game itself was duly going to plan, Liverpool duly piled in goal after goal, but for Josh it wouldn't have mattered if it had been a boring game; just being there was so special. Josh was so high on adrenalin he did almost let his guard slip near the end when getting carried away and momentarily forgetting what year he was in, said "I can't believe we lost to this lot in the FA cup semi-final!"

Peter was puzzled, "What the heck are you on about?" Josh realised his error immediately.

"Just messing with you," he quietly reassured his father soon after the final whistle blew. Liverpool 9, Crystal Palace 0.

"We'll have to go to more matches if they play like this!" enthused Peter Stanton. "Of course, I'd like nothing better and if you keep beating me at pool, I'll keep paying!" replied a very contented Josh. Knowing his deep knowledge of Liverpool history, especially a season where Liverpool won their last Championship, would hold him in good stead. A special friendship had been sealed. Josh was so happy and contented and so caught up in the moment that being stuck in the past wasn't a problem, was he even bothered about trying to figure out how to get back to the rightful time? How long could he resist telling his dad who he really was?

Chapter 4

Living Memory

During the months of October and November 1989, Josh Stanton was still enjoying the life and times of this era and was impervious to any longing or desire to return or trying to return to his era, having knowledge of how events turn out was so powerful and rewarding and to all intents and purposes, Josh was living the dream. He was living history.

Josh's friendship with his dad was steadily strengthening over time and he would experience lots of Liverpool matches during these months with his father, the highlight being at Goodison Park to see Liverpool win 3-1 at Everton on the 23rd September 1989.

"Sweet, truly sweet," Josh rapturously enthused. It was on this day he encountered a certain Tommy Brown, Ryan Brown's dad. That got Josh wondering about Ryan but he felt reassured that Ryan was probably okay. Seeing Ryan's dad so young was just as astonishing as seeing his own dad in this time. Josh knew Tommy was a very passionate Evertonian so declined to approach him, but Josh admired Tommy all the same as Josh knew

Tommy Brown had brought up Ryan as a single father and Ryan loved his father just as much as Josh loved his father. It was just that in future Josh's father was cruelly taken away, but Ryan had grown up not knowing his mother as she apparently left Tommy when Ryan was just a toddler so they could empathise with each other.

Undoubtedly the worst game during this time for Josh was a 4-1 defeat at Southampton in October, it was a shocker and it took place at the dell, a tight and claustrophobically small, antiquated ground.

"I'm glad that place will be confined to history," moaned Josh. Josh was beginning to appreciate how much football grounds had to be improved and how lucky he had been to go so many vastly improved stadiums in his time. Josh really wanted to disclose to his dad the secrets of the future, he wanted to tell his dad all about Istanbul.

Istanbul, of course, was the epic scene of a truly inspirational and wonderful champions league final win for Liverpool against AC Milan, Liverpool showing incredible fighting spirit to come from 0-3 behind at half time to somehow get the game back to 3-3 and an eventual penalty shoot-out triumph. How Josh would have loved to see the unbridled joy on his dad's face at such an iconic triumph against all the odds. How Josh yearned for his dad to share this exquisite moment later in his life! Josh also didn't depress his dad by telling him to make the most of this seasons. This year's Championship (1990) would be the last title Liverpool would win for at least the next 25 years. It was getting so very frustrating having to bite his lip, above everything else Josh wanted to warn his dad about what was going to befall him in 1998, but he didn't know how his own situation was going to evolve.

Another memorable game, for the wrong reasons for Josh, was in November 1989. Millwall 1, Liverpool 2. Great win but, oh my god, those Millwall fans! Josh had never felt so intimidated all his life, he had just experienced a trip to the "Old Den", Millwall's notorious former home. Nothing had prepared him for the threatening, foreboding area of South East London. Cold Blow Lane was such an apt name. This brought home to him the dark, violent overtones of this era and how hooliganism was a much darker menace back then. Josh realised how much things had gotten better in his time and how maybe he took it for granted.

There was one game where Josh wasn't accompanied by his dad and that was at the end of November 1989, Sheffield Wednesday 0, Liverpool 2. Sheffield Wednesday's ground, Hillsborough, had been the scene of a horrific and calamitous tragedy earlier that year involving Liverpool fans losing their lives in terrible scenes of overcrowding in the Leppings Lane area of the ground, seeing people crushed to death. Peter Stanton couldn't bring himself to go to this game so Josh went alone to that one. Josh was well and truly living history and was getting well immersed in this era of the game. December 1989 came quickly round and there were 3 games that month that Josh was looking forward to: Manchester City away, Chelsea away and the nemesis, Manchester United at home on the 23rd December 1989.

Josh was looking forward to the away days at Manchester City and Chelsea as both these clubs were both very rich clubs in the year 2010 and Josh was eager to find out what life was like for them in the year 1989. Josh knew Manchester City played their games at Maine Road, back then and not at their plush Etihad Stadium, visiting Manchester on this 2nd December, Josh was intrigued to see Maine Road nestled amongst the terraced street of Moss Side.

"This is going to be Millwallesque," mused Josh. He had read all the stories about Moss Side and its alleged violent surroundings. Josh was well impressed at the sight of the Kippax and would end up being made up with a good day all round as Liverpool duly coasted to another victory: Manchester City 1, Liverpool 4, with the mighty Ian Rush scoring 2 goals.

Two weeks later was the much anticipated visit to Chelsea and its Stamford Bridge ground. In the year 2010 Josh knew how rich and successful a club Chelsea were with an impressive ground with its Chelsea village complex accompanying it, Josh was going to be in for a shock at what he saw. Stamford Bridge was nothing like he knew it; it was so incredibly disappointing! There were 2 barren, open terraces at either end set what seemed miles from the pitch and another mundane stand down one side, leaving just one giant stand on the eastern side that he could recognise, which stood out like a beacon in such a downbeat venue. The atmosphere would just dissipate away in the environment but things were going to get better as once again Josh was there to see another Liverpool master class, as Liverpool strolled to a convincing victory with another 2 goals from the mighty Ian Rush. Chelsea 2, Liverpool 5. Now for the visit next week of Manchester United to Josh's beloved Anfield.

Saturday 23rd December 1989, Liverpool v Manchester United, was the day that Josh's comfortable existence in this era would start to become uneasy; the first seeds of a troubling slide in Josh's world would be sown in his mind. It was all sparked by the arrival of Manchester United and seeing a certain Mark Robins within their party. This ignited Josh's realisation that he was in a critical phase of football history; Manchester United arrived at Anfield in an ordinary mid-table position and a lot of his fellow Liverpool fans were wallowing in their rivals mediocrity, but Josh wasn't wallowing with them as that sight of Mark Robins was a sobering one, as he knew how important Mark Robins was going to be in just 2 weeks' time. Mark Robins was going to score a goal of monumental importance and a whole almighty powerful dynasty of Manchester United under Mr Ferguson would be involved.

"You're very quiet today," noticed Peter Stanton.

"Just thinking how much I hate united," said Josh, starting to realise how to put in a plan to stop this evolution and keep Liverpool firmly well out of

Manchester United's reach. This whole undercurrent of feelings would overshadow Josh's enjoyment of this usual blood and thunder occasion, but there wasn't really anything to get excited about in this game as it just petered out into a goalless stalemate: Liverpool 0, Manchester United 0. Josh wasn't too upset about this dull game, Josh was now focussed on what he could do to stop Manchester United, stop Mark Robins and somehow take him out of action.

Chapter 5

Careful What You Wish For

December 31st 1989, New Year's Eve and everything until now for Josh in this time had been exciting. Josh loved being in the company of his dad and had been very clever in not doing anything that he might live to regret if he ever went back to his own time. Josh knew from his science and physics grounding that something profound caused by himself in 1989 could radically change the future, Josh knew this wasn't linear but could spear off in a tangent into a really different reality, but Josh's obsessive hatred of Manchester United was binding him to this danger as he focussed on his plan to stop Mark Robins and jeopardise the future success of Manchester United.

Being New Year's Eve, the beers were flowing at their local club. Even though he was 17, Josh looked a couple of years older, so Josh had no problem commandeering a considerable amount of alcohol. This was a monumental error of judgement; as the beers flowed Josh's sound judgement and reasoning were being lowered. The only awkward times Josh had to address before this night were the times Josh saw his dad with his mum, as he had turned up that first day and he was perceived to be acting weird by his future mother, but Josh had easily got round this by insisting he thought it was his auntie's house.

The rendition of 'Auld Lang Syne' would herald an outbreak of emotion and a terrible loss of inhibition from normally such a well-disciplined Josh Stanton.

"I love you, Dad, I really love you," Peter Stanton was horrified.

"What the hell are you on about?"

Josh proceeded to hug Peter Stanton, giving him a tight squeeze. "Off me, you weirdo! Don't come near me again!"

Josh was absolutely mortified; he had made a right fool of himself and had severely compromised his relationship with his dad, all this made him want to consume more alcohol, especially seeing Peter Stanton and his mother leave the premises with indecent haste, but Josh wouldn't be alone for long; someone was taking an interest.

Unbeknown to Josh, an attractive blonde haired beauty had been sizing him up for most of the night and could now sense her opportunity to get to know him.

"Looks like you could do with some company," she enthusiastically pronounced.

"I've blown it big time," replied a crestfallen Josh.

"Don't worry, I'll take care of you, just buy me a drink and I'll brush all your sorrows away." Josh was in no mood to resist such a welcome offer and his urge to forget the pain of upsetting his dad and the suffering of rejection with such an attractive accomplice to compensate was leading to one conclusion.

"Come on, you can come home with me."

This mysterious lady eagerly offered and Josh duly obliged. 1990 was going to begin with a whole heap of trouble! Josh didn't realise blonde haired beauty was a originally destined to meet a certain Tommy Brown that night and this beauty would be destined to give birth to Ryan. By going home with her, she never met Tommy and so there would be no Ryan Brown but this was just the tip of the iceberg to what would await Josh Stanton if he ever got back to 2010.

1st January 1990. Waking up in a strange bed brought the cold sobering realisation of the previous evening. Being present in this time was losing its appeal if he had lost the friendship and respect of his father. Josh was fond of the beauty he had met last night but didn't feel like romance in the light of his heartache. Josh made his excuses and left. He did want to attend to other business, namely it was New Year's Day and Liverpool were playing away at Nottingham Forest, the very same Nottingham Forest that would play host to Manchester United in that very important FA cup tie in just 6 days' time.

This wasn't going to be just a football match today, for Josh it was going to be a fact finding mission!

As it transpired this match was an exciting end to an affair amongst 2 good teams nestled in this quaint stadium situated by the River Trent. Josh couldn't believe how Nottingham Forest would get knocked out of the cup next week but he knew it would happen unless he tried to do something about it, all this did was crystallise Josh's determination to scupper Manchester United, changing history and its consequences was only secondary to his compulsive desire to see Manchester United suffer. As the final whistle sounded on this exciting match it was Nottingham Forest 2, Liverpool 2.

Josh had come up with a plan of action and he called it "Operation Carrington".

Josh knew Manchester United trained at Carrington Training Complex situated to the south west of Manchester. Josh decided to vigilantly keep a keen eye on all the coming and going of the players from the complex, hoping to see which car belonged to Mark Robins and devise a way of intercepting Mark and sabotaging him, so that he would miss the Nottingham Forest game.

By the Wednesday of that week, Josh knew the route Mark Robins would use out of the complex and put his cunning plan into action. He saw Mark Robins coming down the road when suddenly Josh collapsed feigning an asthma attack, Mr Robins duly stopped the car and asked if he was alright and if there was anything he could do. Josh asked to be taken to a chemist, sensing this was the golden opportunity he prayed for. Josh asked Mr Robins to go into the chemist for him, knowing he would wait outside the shop and execute his cunning plan. It worked a treat, Mr Robins duly proceeded to leave the shop when he tripped over Josh Stanton's outstretched leg, strategically placed to provide maximum impact, Mr Robins was never expecting to encounter such an occurrence and duly tumbled awkwardly onto the concrete pavement. "Oh my god, my knee!"

"What's up with it?" asked Josh, coming over all concerned with feigned sincerity.

"It's twisted, I'm in a lot of pain!"

Josh continued his mock concern and replied, "Gosh I'm so sorry! I'll ring an ambulance for you. Hope you're going to be okay and right for the cup game," knowing that was now going to be unlikely. Josh's plan had worked!

Sunday 7th January 1990, Nottingham Forest v Manchester United in the 3rd round of the FA cup. Josh Stanton settled down to watch the game on the television. Both team's line-ups were announced and there was no mention of Mark Robins anywhere. Josh waited to see what would happen with breathless anticipation, as originally intended the match was proving a tight affair, no goals and Nottingham Forest putting on loads of pressure. It was getting near to full time and Manchester United broke away and created their golden chance but this time the chance went begging, Mark Robins was not there to score. The commentator duly noted, "We're told Mark Robins, who would've played today, suffered a knee injury in midweek and is out for 2 to

3 weeks, I think he would have probably done better with that chance."

Soon after, the final whistle blew: Nottingham Forest 0, Manchester United 0. History had been changed for now but what would the replay produce?

This replay was uncharted territory; Josh Stanton should have been happy but strangely, now that history had altered, Josh felt increasingly uneasy and he now realised how silly he might have been. Josh was expecting to be triumphantly ecstatic but he didn't feel that; he was quite scared, scared that everything he was used to might now change! He was wrapped up in his crusade; he hadn't stopped to think of the consequences and the super charged adrenalin he had been feasting on to Nottingham Forest. His misdemeanours of New Year's Eve were ebbing away, for the first time since his arrival in 1989, Josh Stanton felt alone. Josh Stanton was feeling trepidation; maybe what he'd done won't prove too costly if Manchester United win the replay but everything now was new territory, history was being rewritten!

Wednesday 10th January 1990, Manchester United v Nottingham Forest 3rd round of the FA cup replay. Still no Mark Robins in the side. Manchester United were desperate to preserve their season and keep their manager safe and were playing much better football, but just couldn't make their pressure tell, wave upon wave the red devils plastered the Forest goal to no avail and then with 1 minute to go, the unthinkable was about to happen. Forest caught

United on the counter-attack, United had left too many players up-field and the ball was played into Nigel Clough's path. He jinked the ball into the net: Manchester United 0, Nottingham Forest 1. There was hardly any time left and the referee blew his whistle. Manchester United were out of the FA cup! A cup they were supposed to win! The rewriting of history was now an unstoppable juggernaut! The ramifications could be huge!

"Oh my god! What have I done?" Josh Stanton was frozen with fear. The damage had been done and was irreversible. Josh Stanton had been incredibly stupid and he knew it, from now on anything could happen; how would history rewrite itself? Josh Stanton certainly didn't know but now there was proof history could be changed. Josh Stanton was deeply ashamed of himself for being what might be catastrophically stupid. The delight of United's demise was dampened by what it all might mean. Now Josh Stanton knew he could no longer hang around in 1990 and knew he had to try and get back to his own time; he didn't want to create more damage to what he already had done, although now that history could be unwritten the temptation to warn his dad about his future fate was overwhelming.

The consequences of Josh Stanton's time changing actions didn't take long to materialise. The headline in the papers indicated 'Alex Ferguson Sacked by Manchester United'. Josh Stanton was happy at that, but knew it wasn't supposed to be like that and to be truthful was more terrified now everything was unravelling at a rate of knots, Josh Stanton's mind was more set than ever on trying to find a way back and there was only one person he could think of who might be able to help him: Xavier Richardson.

Xavier Richardson was the tutorial master of science and physics at Manchester College. Josh Stanton had the utmost regard for Xavier's knowledge and know-how in this field and had spent a very enjoyable time studying under his stewardship. The trouble was where to find Mr Richardson in this time; all Josh knew was Xavier Richardson was in his late fifties in 2010 so Mr Richardson would be approaching forty, or at least his late thirties.

Josh tried hard to think of any clues of where to look and any one distinctive thing he could remember. Then he realised Mr Richardson had a distinctive Middlesboro accent so a good starting point would be to go to Middlesboro and see if he could pinpoint a Xavier Richardson. Not many people's name begin with an X so it shouldn't be hard, Josh just hoped Mr Xavier Richardson, if he found him, would have gained the knowledge and expertise to provide plausible answers to what Josh had experienced.

Josh didn't have to wait long to find him once he got to Middlesboro – there were plenty of Richardson's but only 1 X Richardson. Josh was very nervous as to how to approach him and didn't want to come across as being perceived to be mad, but was confident the Mr Richardson he knew would be open minded. Josh was also nervous he would laugh at Xavier's voice as it was so much like Marcus Bentley from *Big Brother*. Josh didn't want him to feel insulted or he most certainly wouldn't help him. Knocking on Xavier's door wasn't going to be easy bit needed to be done.

"Hello, can I help you?" answered Mr Richardson.

"I hope so, I certainly hope so!" exclaimed Josh

"What about?" Mr Richardson asked, Josh Stanton took a deep breath.

"I know you're going to find this hard to believe, but I'm trapped in the past, I'm from the future and know you through being your student at Manchester College, I know you have an extensive knowledge of metaphysics and believe you might be the only person I know who might be able to help me." Josh waited breathlessly for a response.

"So, tell me, how did you get into this predicament?" was Xavier Richardson's reply, at least reassuringly he hadn't written Josh off as a crank.

"There was this strange bubble-like sphere of light emanating from this house in Liverpool which I entered rather stupidly, albeit briefly, and when I re-emerged here I was in 1989." said Josh, waiting for Mr Richardson to shoot him down, but his response surprised Josh.

"Well, well, well I thought this was completely theoretical!"

"What is? What is?" asked a quizzical Josh.

"In essence, a time bubble, an area of distorted time in the space time continuum, but like any bubbles, they can burst then reform, trouble is–"

"–What? What's the trouble?" enquired Josh.

"You should be dead, or at the very least badly shocked, and you shouldn't have been able to infiltrate this bubble," Mr Richardson continued. "I can't understand how you could get to be here, any contact with this bubble would have given off a powerful discharge and repelled you a long way, let alone you entering it. I need to test you for a temporal reading to determine your claims; I'm sceptical, to say the least."

Josh Stanton readily agreed knowing what he was saying was the truth. Xavier Richardson sounded reassuringly knowledgeable and open minded so there was hope. As predicted the temporal test showed Josh Stanton's body 20 years out of temporal synch.

"Wow, you're telling the truth! But I still don't know how you managed to infiltrate the bubble, do you have anything abnormal about you?" asked Mr Richardson.

"There's only one thing that might be slightly abnormal," admitted Josh.

"Tell me, what is that?"

"I do have AB negative blood, which only 1% of white Caucasians possess and I'm told it's even less in other ethnic groups, I know this as I looked it up on the internet."

"What's the internet?" asked Mr Richardson. "On second thought, don't tell me too much information of the future; it could prove to be very harmful. Aanyway, your blood might be the answer to this conundrum. It is not beyond the realms of possibility that having a certain type of blood might allow for it to have an earthing effect, negating any problems that barrier discharge would present. This would allow you to pass through – you are very lucky though."

"Wouldn't say that," argued Josh.

"Oh you are! Like I said, you could've quite easily been killed, you're like one in a million almost, I've got an interesting analogy."

"What's that?" asked Josh.

"It's like the sperm and the egg analogy; so many sperm but only a tiny percentage get to penetrate the barrier. You're one of the tiny percentage."

"Thanks for that analogy." Josh sincerely meant, but the pressing question remained for him.

"Will this bubble re-appear and where and when?"

"That's going to take a lot of working out, like I said I thought they were theoretical, I'll need to make a lot of mathematical equations, I'll get back to you on that, in the meantime you must not do anything to radically alter anything in this time or you will face a potentially radically different future," said a stern Mr Richardson.

"Why's that?" asked Josh, knowing full well what he had done, but hoping Mr Richardson's prognosis wouldn't be as potentially catastrophic as Josh suspected it might. He was hoping for a bit of comfort, but Mr Richardson's reply chilled him to the bone.

"I'll give you another analogy of a car windscreen that's fully intact, that represents the timeline that was taking its natural course. If someone or something happens to alter the natural course of time, however, minuscule things will be creating small chips in the windscreen, a chink or imperfection can lead to a calamitous shattering of the whole windscreen over a period of time if left unrepaired. Therefore, the origin of just a small chink in the natural timeline is spread an inordinate amount of splinters of fractured timelines and altered occurrences which leads to an eventual shattering of the natural timeline that you are used to. It can result from that one little chip or imperfection, you can see why you absolutely must be extremely careful, don't you?" Josh just gulped and nodded, not wanting to disclose to Mr Richardson what he had done, he felt too ashamed to do this and frightened of how Mr Richardson would react. Mr Richardson agreed to contact Josh when he had more information to give him. Would he be able to give Josh hope he would get back okay? And what might be in store for Josh if he did get back? Would Josh be brave enough to admit what he'd done to Mr Richardson in due course? Would Mr Richardson be right in his assertion that the future would be radically different to anything Josh had previously known?

Chapter 6

In Times of Trouble

Two weeks of agonising had passed and not a word from Mr Xavier Richardson. Josh Stanton was keeping a low profile and had lost his appetite for going to any football matches, being unsure of how his actions were going to play out, he just wasn't as keen anymore. Josh Stanton was eager for answers. This was about to come; the eagerly anticipated call duly arrived on 1st February 1990.

"Can you come and see me? I think I have some information for you," urged Mr Richardson.

"Thank you, is it good news? Josh nervously uttered.

"If my calculation is right, I think it's positive," was the promising response.

Josh Stanton's heart was beating fast and furiously – he was puzzled why Mr Richardson needed to see him but was comforted that he was going to see him and not just impart information over the phone. This was going to be the most eagerly awaited meeting of Josh Stanton's life; it meant everything, he couldn't get there quick enough.

"Hello Josh, good to see you again, if I'm right the next time I see you will be in 20 years' time." Mr Richardson's welcome was music to Josh's ears.

"Sounds like very positive news, have you got a time and date?"

"I believe this time bubble, as you want to call it, will appear again on 1st March 1990 in the same place, but please be warned I believe it will be there for a very short window of time and if you miss it you will not get back to your time as I have an analogy for you."

"Oh, not another one," said Josh, only half joking.

"It's the buses analogy, you can wait hours for one and then 2 will appear almost together. In terms of cosmic time, 20 years is as good as together but when I speak of hours in cosmic terms, you are talking thousands of years apart from these 2 occurrences. This will not happen again in your lifetime." Mr Richardson confirmed, "Oh and another thing… don't spend too long inside the bubble. Remember you stepped out after only roughly half a minute; if you stay in too long you will overshoot 2010 and appear well into the future." Mr Richardson's warning was chilling, this was incredibly serious stuff. Mr Richardson tried to lighten the tone by liking the bubble back to the buses analogy in the way that 1989/2010 was a like a bus stop in time amongst hundreds of bus stops going throughout space-time, but Josh wasn't seeing a funny side to it; he was chilled to the bone! But Josh was very grateful for Mr Richardson's help.

"Thank you so much, I owe you everything," he said.

"That's alright, I've found the whole thing enriching and challenging!" Mr Richardson replied.

"Can I ask you another question?" asked Josh "Can you have 2 different versions of yourself in the same time?"

"No I don't think so, I believe you will fuse into the version you're supposed to be in that moment in time," was Mr Richardson's reply. "I think if you stepped out of that bubble in the year 1997, for example, I believe you would have moulded into your 4 year old self." Mr Richardson added, "I've got analogy for you."

"Oh no, not another one!" replied Josh.

"I know you like them really," responded a thoughtful Mr Richardson. "Think of a Tarzan zip-wire ride at a water park. You are travelling along the zip-wire which represents you at this minute, but at some point you will meet a block on the zip-wire which makes you lose your grip on the zip-wire and releases you from it. The zip-wire represents the timeline and the block you meet is your natural conception. So you can see, this block will see you release your grip on the timeline in the form that you see now, meaning you would fade from existence."

"Wow, what about if you did something in the past that you shouldn't have, what then?" said Josh, not being able to put off his terrifying curiosity of what was in store for him, Mr Richardson was candid and scarily straight to the point.

"I've told you before: potentially catastrophic!"

"I hope I haven't done anything!"

"Nothing for you would be certain, you might just not even exist now in the year 2010, if reality has changed, the world you knew is not the one waiting for you." With this chilling prophecy, Josh again thanked Mr Richardson and left. He knew what he needed to know: he'd already altered the timeline so the question now was: would he go any further and address the issues of trying to make sure his dad would not befall his fatal accident of 1998 before he took his leap of faith into that bubble? One thing was sure, if he didn't go back he only had just over 2 years to live as a teenager as he was due to be conceived by his mother sometime in the summer of 1992 and if what Mr Richardson said was correct, Josh would mould into his embryotic self: there was no choice!

Josh agonised greatly over what to do with his dad but eventually plucked up the courage to confront this issue. It was very difficult but his dad meant everything to him and he couldn't pass up the opportunity to warn him about 1998. If Josh was going to go back to 2010, he wanted his dad to be there in the future, the future reality was already going to be different and Josh was prepared to risk making it even more different for the sake of his dad. This wasn't going to be easy to talk to his dad as Peter had took great umbrage at Josh on New Year's Eve, feeling he had been completely ridiculed. Peter Stanton had kept well away from Josh for the last few weeks. Although he was sorry he made his dad feel bad, Josh felt fully justified in having his say. Josh plucked up all the courage he could muster and knocked on his father's door and then waited nervously for it to open.

"Oh not you again, I told you not to bother me again! Clear off!" was the stern greeting awaiting Josh.

"Don't worry, I'm leaving in a few days. I have to explain myself to you before I go."

"Why? You showed me up in front of the whole club, making me a laughing stock. I can't show my face in there, what have you got to say that will make up for that? I'm only 5 years older than you I thought we were going to be best mates and then you just go and completely spoil everything! I think you need some psychiatric help!" said an ashen faced Peter Stanton, who was in no mood for conciliatory speech.

"I don't expect you to believe that you're my dad, like you said, how could you be? It does sound like nonsense and I know you'll think I'm crazy when I tell you I'm from the future, but I am and you are my dad. I've come to see you today as I hope to go back to my time and I need to tell you about something that's going to happen to you in the future," reasoned Josh. Peter Stanton was just about to slam the door on Josh's face.

"You really do need some help! You've had your say, now just go away and don't come back or I'll do something I regret!" said an irate Peter at the end of his tether. Josh had only one trick left up his sleeve.

"Just let me give you this, maybe one day you'll believe me and know that somehow I was telling you the truth," pleaded Josh, proceeding to get his wallet out and pluck his prized photograph of himself and his dad playing football together in the garden. "Please keep this. I promise I'm going now and I won't bother you again, but before I go, I'll just give you a few tips so you might realise all this is the truth and I'm not crazy. All I will say is it would pay you to take great interest in people like Phil Taylor and Stephen Hendry as they will become multi world champions, and oh, I almost forgot, Crystal Palace will knock Liverpool out of the FA cup 4-3 in the semi-final." Josh was in full flow talking with reckless carefree abandon while Peter Stanton just stood transfixed at the photograph he had been given. Josh sensed the chance to put across the one thing he needed to. "On December 15th 1998, please don't venture out in your car; you're going to have an accident." Josh didn't know if this registered with his dad. He could see his dad looked visibly shaken, but Josh knew he'd done all he could. "I'm going now, I'm sorry to put this all on you but I needed to as I…" Josh was going to say "love you", but thought it wasn't wise in the circumstances.

"What were you going to say?" said Peter Stanton, slowly coming around from his stasis of disbelief, "I was, I was… going to say," Josh stuttered, "please look after Jane" he wasn't going to say his mother in case it antagonised his father again. "I know she's really going to be into this new group called Take That, so indulge her if you have to and don't get too upset like Gazza when we lose penalties in the world cup semi-final to Germany," Josh suddenly realised he was going much too far and had to stop, he just so wanted to reel off events so his dad might just realise they were true and therefore take into account what Josh had said about his dad's fatal accident of December 1998. Josh didn't know the true effect of giving Peter Stanton his prized photograph, for all he knew Peter might not believe that child in the photograph was a young Josh Stanton, but Josh knew he had very much given Peter Stanton food for thought. It was time to go. Josh said a tearful, emotional goodbye and left, all he could do now was hope. The focus now was most definitely on leaving this time and seeing what was waiting for him at the other end.

March 1st 1990 came round quickly, too quickly for Josh's liking, but Josh knew this was it, the day of destiny. That's if Mr Xavier Richardson's calculations were correct. Josh walked across Stanley Park towards Anfield Road and his beloved Liverpool football club. Walking across Stanley Park all those really competitive local football matches with all his mates was jogged into Josh's memory, as he looked back, Goodison Park was just about to be hidden from his view behind some woodland. All the focus now was going forward, forward to hopefully renewing old acquaintances especially with his best friend, Ryan Brown and having all the verbal banter with the Evertonians renewed. Josh Stanton approached the dim, boarded up houses of the derelict area behind Liverpool's main stand and gazed nervously around him with a yearning anticipation.

"Oh, please be right! Please be right! Please let me see signs that the bubble is there!" True to form, behind the last boarded up house the tell-tale glow of emanating light was seen protruding inside. Josh was so incredibly nervous as he scrambled to find a way inside this boarded house which he duly achieved and there it was as predicted… The same bubble that had given him this adventure. Josh Stanton composed himself and took a massive sharp intake of breath.

"Remember Josh, just a few seconds, count to fifteen and then leave it, that should do it," Josh mumbled to himself as he approached this momentous moment of truth.

Josh duly proceeded to manage to infiltrate the barrier of the bubble just as before, but there was something slightly different this time. Josh Stanton felt some pain in doing so, there was definitely a tingling sensation inside him this time. Josh Stanton hadn't felt that last time, but just shook the feeling off and promptly stayed inside to the count of fifteen and then promptly stepped out again. Was this it? Was he back in 2010? And what was the world like that was waiting for him?

Chapter 7

A New Reality Bites

Josh Stanton expected to re-merge in the same boarded up house that he entered but having stepped out of the bubble it was clear he was back in his bedroom. His first thoughts were of an overwhelming sense of relief in still being alive and grateful that he still existed. His eyes nervously panned around the room for any signs of radical change. His bedroom was still a shrine to his beloved Liverpool, containing lots of memorabilia but there was no longer that prized poster of Steven Gerrard, Jamie Carragher and the rest of the Liverpool team celebrating winning in Istanbul.

"Where's that gone?" puzzled Josh. Then his eyes fixed on the Liverpool calendar. It was showing April 2010, so Josh assumed that he was back a month before he originally left. As he studied the calendar he was taken aback at the lack of familiar faces on it. He hardly recognised any of them! "Where's Stevie G? Where's Torres or Jamie Carragher?" said Josh, starting to get a bit disconcerted. Josh was nervous very, very nervous and even more so when noticing his laptop was no longer there. Josh was going to have to go down to the library and go online there if he was to catch up with events and come to terms with what had changed. "Probably just a bit has changed" Josh comforted himself. Then another unsettled thought in his head, 'I hope there still is internet.'

Josh took a massive deep breath and prepared to go downstairs and face the world.

"Hello Josh, have you had a nice day?" said the welcomingly reassuring voice of his mother. Josh looked so relieved his mother was still there. "You look all pale Josh are you alright?" asked his mother, noticing how Josh was looking strange. Josh, having got through one hurdle, then prepared to ask his mother the massively important question about his dad, was he still alive?

"How's Dad today and where is he?" asked Josh with nervous trepidation. Had his rendezvous with his dad had the desired effect? Had it worked? He waited for the answer with baited breath.

"Oh, Josh you know where your dad is, he's going to be in care for a long time! Motor Neurone Disease just doesn't go away you know!" was his mother's devastating reply.

Josh Stanton was horror struck! All that effort to save him from his original fate had led to another tragic circumstance. Josh was devastated at the turn of events; he felt truly responsible. He so loved his dad and was mortified that his dad was suffering such a crippling disease. His mother noticed the tears welling in his eyes. "I know, Josh, it never gets any easier does it? We just have to be strong." Josh didn't feel like being strong, he couldn't look at himself in the mirror after this, Josh knew he was going to burst into floods of tears, so quickly made an exit strategy.

"Just need to pop out to the shops."

"Okay, but make sure you avoid those Evertonian lads," his mother replied. Josh was perplexed!

"Why do I need to avoid them? I've always had a good rapport with them, I've always enjoyed winding them up!" Perhaps his mother had got too over protective. "My best friend Ryan Brown is a passionate Evertonian and we always have a good crack, can't wait to see him again," mused Josh, unaware that one of his actions in the past meant Ryan Brown didn't exist in this timeline. Josh Stanton opened his front door and was immediately in no doubt that things were not the same as he had left… "Where's Goodison Park? It's vanished!" said a badly startled Josh. No Goodison Park Football Ground! It had gone! Instead a nice little plush group of houses stood where Goodison Park proudly stood for all those many years, Josh stared at the road sign… Carragher Way! "This most definitely doesn't look good!" agonised Josh, already realising he wasn't liking this timeline he'd come back to. It was going to get worse, much worse!

Josh proceeded to cut across Stanley Park and was soon to be taken aback with the breath-taking sight that was to await him, right in the middle of Stanley Park was no longer the playing pitches he so loved to play football on with his mates, but a massively spectacular state of the art football stadium. Josh knew this was what Liverpool always wanted, had they finally achieved it? His eyes locked on with mortifying horror at the words emblazoned high up on the massively impressive North stand… Everton FC! "Oh no! Please no! Please let his be a horrible dream! Please!" panicked a horrified Josh Stanton, then a crumb of comfort came into his mind, 'it's probably the ground share they didn't want to happen.' Josh perused all the signs of the ground for any sign of red, for anything that would signify that Liverpool Football Club were also owners of such an impressive stadium, a stadium that was bigger and better than Old Trafford, the home of Manchester United and a place that could hold over 75,000 people. 'This ground must hold at least 80,000 people! It's got to include Liverpool FC as Everton wouldn't be able to fill it!' thought Josh, trying to rationalise this unfathomable situation. Alas, all around the ground displayed the blue of Everton, there was no sign of red or anything Liverpool FC. This was most definitely Everton's Football Ground and just Everton's Football Ground.

"Bloody hell! Looks like they've done really well! There was no way they were in the position to do this before, although I know they've always been a good club, they were always in our shadow and they were always saying they were skint."

Josh knew Everton had prospered but what of the mighty reds? Where were they? Were they still at Anfield or had they got an even more amazing stadium? 'I mean if Everton could get their stadium, Liverpool FC with the massive fan base and worldwide appeal must be somewhere totally mind blowing; perhaps Stanley Park wasn't glamorous enough for the mighty reds,' thought Josh. Josh nervously gazed towards Anfield Road and even though he always maintained that he adored Anfield Stadium, having seen the crowning majesty of Everton's new ground he was gutted that it appeared to be similar, albeit he could just see the top of the Anfield Road end, it didn't appear Liverpool FC had moved, it seemed Liverpool could even be in Everton's shadow. "God forbid that!" protested an unbelieving Josh, "maybe the Kop is really spectacular?" continued Josh, trying to conjure up some enthusiasm. He was going to be very underwhelmed at what he saw; the whole place needed a lick of paint for a start and was in a state of neglect. It looked stale and Josh noticed there weren't so many people walking around the place like he was used to seeing. As Josh proceeded to move around to the Kop end he was not going to get any happier. The ticket office was selling tickets for a League 1 home game against Yeovil Town, Exeter City and Hartlepool United. "What the hell has happened here? Liverpool, in League 1? This is beyond my worst nightmare."

Josh Stanton wanted answers. There was only one place he was heading for and that was the library and the internet, what could have gone so terribly wrong? Josh Stanton had to find out what happened to put such a catastrophic turn of events into reality, was it really all started with the Mark Robins incident? Can one incident really lead to such a devastating state of affairs? Where were Manchester United in the scheme of things? Why the massive rise of Everton? Josh Stanton needed answers!

Accessing the internet, he found they weren't long in coming up top. Everton FC – League Champions 3 times out of the last 4 seasons and reigning Champions League holders having beaten Barcelona 3-1 in the 2009 Champions League final with 2 goals from Cristiano Ronaldo and 1 from Steven Gerrard…

"Steven Gerrard? You've got to be kidding me!

Josh accessed further information… Everton FC… most successful club in the 21st century, great upsurge in results brought about by Sir Alex Ferguson who was appointed manager of Everton FC in 1994. Everton's meteoric rise the result of a personal crusade of Mr Ferguson to prove Manchester United wrong when he was sacked 3 and half years previously and with the infusion of cash mainly from the rich Arabs of Abu Dhabi.

"It's all my fault, it's all my fault, if I hadn't sabotaged Mark Robins then Manchester United wouldn't have sacked Mr Ferguson! What have I done?" Josh was inconsolable at his indiscretion, this was nothing as he surveyed the Everton squad for the 2009-10 season… Buffon, Alves, Carragher, Vidic, Ashley Cole, Gerrard. Alonso, Ronaldo, Fabregas, Torres and Rooney!

‘This is just too much! This is unbelievable! I can believe they would not keep hold of Wayne Rooney but getting Steven Gerrard, Torres and Jamie Carragher from us, I just can’t stomach this! I’ve got to do something to put this right!’ Josh was feeling totally sick, but had to discover more; what happened to Liverpool? Why had they plunged to such depths?

He found Liverpool FC was relegated to League 1 at the end of 2008/09 season with just 25 points, the final indignity of a decline started at the turn of the century when startled at the rise of their rivals Everton and trying to keep up with them. Liverpool overreached themselves resulting in a financial crisis of crippling proportions and necessitating a sale of their star players to ensure survival…

Josh Stanton had read enough! It really was too much to bear and it was all down to him and just to make matters worse, Manchester United were still a prosperous and winning club, although not as prolific as Everton. History had most definitely changed and most definitely it wasn’t for the better, Liverpool’s demise mirrored the Leeds United collapse in the original timeline and Everton had received the cash windfalls from the oil rich Arab sheiks that so prospered Manchester City on the back of a rich run of success generated by Sir Alex Ferguson, who most definitely shouldn’t have been anywhere near being Everton manager as he was destined to be firmly securing the dynasty of Manchester United.

Josh's obsession with trying to stop that dynasty had opened up a massive hornet's nest! It wasn't only the football side of things, Josh was going to discover the enjoyable comforting world he'd left behind in the original timeline wasn't going to be replicated in this new timeline. Josh Stanton had enjoyed all the verbal banter with his Evertonian friends in the original timeline. There was an affable level of affinity between them, mainly facilitated by the fact Ryan Brown, Josh's best friend, was an Evertonian. This cordiality was no longer present as Josh was soon to discover on his way home. A group of Evertonians whom Josh recognised as friendly in the past approached him and their demeanour suggested something a lot more hostile.

"Hey up, Josh! You sad little red! Have you bought your ticket for the mighty Yeovil Town?" said the ringleader with sneering condescension, Josh wasn't used to any level of local hostility before, but he could sense its prevalence now, especially when he was about to cut through Stanley Park on the way home.

"Where do you think you're going? We're not having a poor little red come into our Stanley Park, this is Everton territory! Reds are not welcome! Just stick to that ramshackle shed you call Anfield! You're not worthy of walking past our stadium! While you're at it, when are you and your family going to move from Gwlady's Street? It's embarrassing having a red live there. We're not going to tolerate this for too much longer!" The ringleader was unequivocally threatening; Josh knew the cordiality of the past timeline was not present here. Josh Stanton wasn't going to argue his case at this moment, his focus was to call on the Brown household to try and seek solace with his best friend, Ryan, and try to get to the bottom of this animosity, but any comfort was not going to be found there. Josh nervously knocked on the door only to be met by more unwanted confrontation.

"What the hell do you want? Eff off!" was not the greeting Josh expected from a disturbingly unkempt Tommy Brown, but he needed to speak to Ryan.

"Can I speak to Ryan?" Josh nervously mumbled, but Tommy cut him short.

"Who's Ryan? There's no-one called Ryan living here! I live alone so go before I make you regret knocking on my door!" It was clear that something more had gone badly wrong and Josh needed to go home and clear his head and try and ascertain what to do next and see if there was any redeeming features of this timeline, as it was all looking so horribly wrong. It seemed an absolute no-brainer as to what Josh had to do and that was to go back into the bubble once more and try and undo the wrongs he committed in the past, most especially not to intercept Mark Robins he knew most definitely that was one action that had drastic consequences. The football consequences of his actions were obvious to see, but why was there no Ryan Brown?

There was a sudden dawn of realisation that came rushing upon him about what other major incidents that had happened in the altered past.

"Oh my god! I wonder if it had anything to do with that blonde lady I encountered at the local club on New Year's Eve?" agonised Josh. He couldn't be sure himself, but it was a crushing confirmation of how reckless he had been and not thinking through about the ramifications that such reckless acts provide, Josh was surer than ever that there was a massive pressure and responsibility to be extremely careful if he was ever to rectify past mistakes and restore the original natural timeline and not create any further 'chips' or compound the trouble he'd already caused.

Josh Stanton was soon to find out there was another big negative to this new timeline; he could no longer contact a Xavier Richardson to discuss his predicament. A phone call to Manchester College confirmed to him that they had never had a lecturer there by that name and what's more, it was made clear there was no Josh Stanton studying there either. "Oh no! Don't say I'm intellectually challenged as well in this timeline, I hate to imagine what I'm supposed to be? I'm probably unemployed knowing what this world is like!" It was confirmed that Josh indeed was unemployed. Josh Stanton's mind was made up; he definitely was going to return to the past, "This timeline is simply unbearable! This is not how it's meant to be! I don't want to live like this!"

The longest month of Josh Stanton's life went agonisingly slowly, though from his previous experience Josh knew when and where the bubble would originally appear and that was July 1st 2010. Josh was so ready to leave this terrible reality behind, he couldn't bear to see his dad suffering or not having his best friend around. He certainly did not like being unemployed but most of all the sight of Everton FC totally lording it over his beloved Liverpool and the unbearable smugness and aggression of the Evertonians was too much to bear, especially seeing Liverpool FC in such dire straits as well. During the last month, Everton were duly crowned Premier League Champions again with Manchester United FA cup winners, Liverpool finished tenth place in League 1 losing to Yeovil and Hartlepool in front of crowds of less than 20,000 people. These truly were the worst of times! A truly miserable existence for anyone of the red persuasion! What made it all worse was that Josh Stanton felt truly alone. He no longer enjoyed the friendship of people he knew well and a lot of them had transferred allegiance from red to blue with such a differing level of disparity between them. July 1st couldn't come quick enough.

At long last the day of destiny was to arrive and Josh could leave all this behind. The reassuring emanating glow of the bubble could once again be seen protruding behind the last boarded up house. Josh was so thankful to see it and so thankful that it still existed in such an offbeat location and not out in the open. Josh was glad at least in this respect that both timelines were similar. Josh Stanton took a massive breath and prepared to re-enter the bubble, it hadn't crossed his mind that it was going to be for the last time, but on entering the bubble Josh experienced an intensely sharp level of pain he could hardly bear, but he knew he had to be inside for up to twenty seconds. Anything less and he would re-appear younger but still in the alternate timeline; he had to endure long enough to re-appear in 1989 so he could right the wrongs of the past. The pain was agonising and challenging him to abort and leave the bubble, but somehow Josh summoned the strength from somewhere to achieve the required amount of time he needed to stay in.

"18... 19... 20..." Josh gasped to himself in a tortuously slow countdown of epic proportions. The level of pain was gut wrenchingly high; Josh endured all he could muster until he could take it no more – was the pain going to be worth it? Had he timed everything right? And if so, could he right the wrong of the past? Whatever the circumstances, it had to be 1989 he was re-appearing in and definitely before that infamous New Year's Eve party, let alone tampering with altering Manchester United's destiny. That was the time period when the chip in the natural timeline would become impossible to prevent, shattering into pieces in the future, the New Year's Eve party was the tipping point that was the absolute critical time changing event from which the natural timeline would never reinsert itself. If not corrected the event where Josh unwittingly meddled into making Ryan Brown, his good friend, never being born by preventing the natural course of romance between Tommy Brown and that attractive blonde haired beauty who should've paired up at that party. Josh Stanton staggered out from the bubble, what was going to await him? When and wherein the time stream was he re-appearing?

Chapter 8

Putting the World to Rights

As Josh left the discomfort of the bubble behind, his body wracked with searing pain Josh could hardly catch his breath at the tension he was feeling. What was going to await him now? The answer was going to be instantaneous as he re-entered the past. As before, Josh was no longer in the boarded house, the clearly audible roars of a decibel rich Kop was ringing in his ears. His eyes focussed on the pitch and it was Liverpool v Manchester United and then his eyes turned to the right and it was his beloved dad, Peter Stanton, standing like a true beacon of light right beside him.

"You're very quiet today, are you alright?" he remarked.

"Yes I am now!" replied Josh, relieved to be reacquainted with the much friendlier era.

"You look very pale and you look like you're wincing with pain have you eaten something dodgy?" noticed Peter Stanton.

"Must have," replied Josh before asking, "what's the date today?"

Josh was very confident it was 23rd December 1989, but needed to hear confirmation from his dad.

"You're really out of it today aren't you? You must have had too many drinks as well as some dodgy food! It's the 23rd December." replied a clearly perplexed Peter Stanton.

"1989?" asked Josh.

"Yes of course its 1989! What planet have you come from?" said a bewildered Peter Stanton. Josh was so very relieved he had arrived back in the past in the nick of time. Actually it was probably perfect timing as it was right at the crucial time when things started to unravel quickly. His original journey to the past started there months earlier but Josh was confident he hadn't done anything radically wrong in that initial period, so Josh was trying to focus on this immediate time-frame. He could do nothing else, having transpired a little later than before he knew the original timeline would never be purely the same but at least the history altering act of sabotaging Mark Robins could be put to rights and before that, the New Year's Eve party which would result in the timeline going off at a massive tangent from that point on.

Josh knew he had to be extremely careful with his actions this time as he knew it was very unlikely he could endure another adventure with the bubble, as he suffered terribly this time and next time he hated to think how much worse it could get. The penny had just dropped; Josh might not be able to go back to 2010! He was probably going to be stuck here in the past, but Josh knew he had to still be so very careful so that the foundations would be laid to ensure he could grow up to experience the reality that was meant to be. Josh gulped at the realisation that he might have just 3 years to experience life in his teenage form before he was going to be conceived and meld into that existence. Josh was frozen rigid at the very thought. But he had to regain his composure and refocus on his environment. He was at Anfield again and with his dad. He had to make the most of everything good, live for now, without making any wrong moves. Looking at Mark Robins out on the Anfield pitch was agonising for Josh he knew he had to let things be this time and not try and interfere – he had to let Mark Robins go and do his stuff. He didn't want to, but he'd seen how things could turn out much more unpleasant. Just seeing Mark Robins turned Josh's blood cold, Josh Stanton couldn't enjoy this match and couldn't wait for the final whistle so he could calm himself down and evaluate how to behave in forthcoming events, how to keep everything on an even keel. It was of paramount importance! It meant everything! As the match finished, Josh was reminded by Peter Stanton of the forthcoming New Year's Eve party at their local club.

"See you next week, Josh, can't wait to see you all plastered!" said Peter.

"Yes, can't wait," replied Josh all calmly, but this time Josh knew he couldn't afford to get plastered and lose all his inhibitions. The next week flew by and the New Year's Eve party came around all too quickly, beers were flowing but Josh was strictly on orange juice this time.

"Come on Josh it's New Year's Eve! You've got to have some beers! What's wrong with you?" Urged Peter Stanton, puzzled that Josh wasn't joining in the beer frenzy.

"Getting up early tomorrow so need to be sober, sorry to be boring, I'll make it up another time," replied Josh, he had managed to be controlled this time and duly left the club just after midnight. He was still on good terms with his dad so time, again, was starting to be rewritten. On leaving the club Josh was approached by the same attractive blonde that he encountered last time.

"Hiya, gorgeous! Where do you think you're going? Come back in with me, I'll look after you baby," she invitingly suggested.

"Nah, sorry I'm tired, got to go," replied Josh.

"You're well boring aren't you? Oh well, it's your loss!" said the blonde all dismissively.

"Don't worry I think I'll be able to live with myself, have a nice time in there," came Josh's diplomatic reply, not wanting to antagonise this lady and jeopardise her mood.

Josh gave himself a contented smile, recognition of his resolution that he had just shown. As he walked back to the flat, Josh knew he had undone one of the wrongs he'd committed first time round. 1st January 1990 was now radically different to that first time, no waking up in a strange lady's bed and also no major fall out with his dad over indulging in too much beer consumption resulting in a complete loss of inhibition. Everything felt rosier but there were still other hurdles to overcome, there could be absolutely no room for any complacency whatsoever! His whole future and his beloved Liverpool FC's future was at stake! It was now only six days to go before the tumultuous cup tie between Nottingham Forest and Manchester United, not long to wait but for Josh every day would seem like a month knowing he really had to lie low and not indulge or engage with anybody or anything that might jeopardise his vital mission of putting the world to rights and that most certainly meant not going to Carrington Manchester United's training ground and intercepting Mark Robins again.

7th January 1990 took what seemed an eternity to arrive, but now the day was here, Nottingham Forest v Manchester United in the 3rd round of the FA Cup. Josh put his radio on to get the team news and with total relief it was made known that Mark Robins was in the team; everything seemed to be as it should be! The match progressed in the manner it initially was meant to be with Forest piling on the pressure on a vulnerable United and looking like they could score at any minute. Josh was so nervous, as he knew they shouldn't score otherwise he hadn't been successful in his mission. There was no reason to think that Forest would score as it was meant to be that they didn't, but Forest were playing so well and getting very close and if Forest did score, history was still different and Manchester United were looking in no shape to prevail should that happen. Minutes seemed like hours, but time was ticking on and despite desperate United rear-guard action it was still 0-0. Everything was still on course but United still had to score otherwise it was a replay that wasn't meant to be.

The game entered the last ten minutes. United had hardly been in Forest's penalty area in the second half, they were being thoroughly outplayed, Josh was getting very, very, anxious and was beginning to get very exasperated and doubting how United could score if they weren't even getting into Forest's half of the field!

"For god's sake, just pass the ball to one of your teammates, don't just hoof the ball anywhere! This is terrible," muttered Josh. He couldn't believe this rabble could be capable of winning any trophy in the next few years, let alone being the fantastic trophy laden colossus that they were destined to become, Forest were laying siege to the United goalmouth in the last few minutes, Forest fans were getting ever more fervent in their vocal support behind their team and also taking time out in chastising Manchester United's beleaguered manager, Alex Ferguson.

"Sacked in the morning! You're getting sacked in the morning!" crowed the exuberant crowd of Forest fans, fully expecting their side to score at any minute, surely the constant pressure would bring them the goal they deserve? Manchester United fans could only watch on, stone-faced, they knew their side was hanging on by their fingertips; their patience was being severely tested by their side's limitations.

Incredibly, as Forest forced yet another corner and with all the big men pressing hard to get that elusive winner, United managed to clear the ball under enormous pressure and with too many Forest players still too far further forward, United broke away with 3 players attacking just 2 Forest defenders. The ball was played through with exquisite precision into the path of… Mark Robins! He was through on goal and with tremendous composure, slotted the ball into the corner of the net!

"1-0 to United! Unbelievable! Daylight robbery!" remarked the commentator. Manchester United fans didn't care! They were ecstatic! They were relieved most of all, but all the past negative emotions they were feeling were now eclipsed by the cacophonous sound of jubilation at their side's upturn in fortune. Forest fans could only stand in utter disbelief they were stunned into silence. It was all so unjust! United seemed to be divinely protected. Forest tried so hard to get an equaliser in the limited time remaining but all to no avail, the final whistle blew and history had been restored! It was totally mixed feelings for Josh; he didn't want United to prosper but it was still much better than the hornets' nest opened up in the alternative timeline. Later that day Josh had further reason to be joyful as passing him down the road was the sight of a loving couple walking hand in hand, it was Tommy Brown and that attractive blonde haired lady he'd met at the New Year's Eve party. Josh gave out a contented smile and moved on, Josh was full of pensive thought as he pondered what to do now in the time he had remaining in the past. He could still undo all his good work if he wasn't still extremely careful! So much so, Josh decided he needed to move away from the Liverpool area to eradicate any possibility of directly affecting the natural course of events. It had to be this way, it was for the best, but first Josh wanted to see his dad, Peter, one last time.

9th January 1990 was to be the final time in this period that Josh was going to see his dad before heading on his way down to pastures new. It was going to be so emotional for him, so sad but everything had to be kept in check for everyone's sake. Josh wanted to intoxicate himself into this moment, to cherish this moment to the maximum as it was going to be so surreal to think that the next time he would see his dad, if his resolve held true, would be in the future, as a child growing up and it would all be too brief, far too brief. Josh would only be 5 years old and nowhere near being able to garnish much discernible memories of his dad when his dad was due to be killed in a fatal car accident, a greatly treasured life cut so unfairly, brutally short but at least avoiding the barbaric cruelty of a life dealing with Motor Neurone Disease. As Josh approached his dad's house this one last time, tears in his eyes were desperately trying to undermine his determination to suppress any excess emotion at the salient occasion. Josh paused at the door whilst he wrestled with regaining his composure, took a deep breath and knocked on the door and waited for his dad to appear.

"Hello Josh, haven't seen you for over a week ever since the New Year's party, how have you been?" greeted a friendly Peter Stanton.

"Oh, fine! Just been staying in and behaving myself," replied Josh, desperately trying not to betray his inner feeling of turmoil.

"I can believe that, you're such a lightweight aren't you? I mean fancying refusing to join in with all that major beer consumption! You'd never cope being related to me!" mocked Peter. Josh just nodded and laughed. If only Peter knew the truth; but he wasn't going to know this time. Josh wanted this last meeting to be non-controversial.

"Peter, I have something to tell you, I'm leaving the area tomorrow so I wanted to say goodbye."

"Oh no, I was enjoying being your friend, I'll miss you at the Liverpool matches. Do you have to go? Where will you be going? I was just getting to know you, I thought there was a good connection between us," replied a genuinely upset Peter.

Josh was in danger of caving into his emotions at such a heart-warming response, but steeled himself to tell Peter that it was for the best and that he would miss Peter a lot and that he would keep in touch, but knowing it would hurt him too much to see him again and there was too much to lose, too much to jeopardise. It had to like this, Josh did want to give Peter one little morsel of information before he left. He couldn't help himself, but wanted to cleverly camouflage this information as an innocent, throwaway, chance remark and maybe his dad would benefit if he believed him enough. He would make a bit of money at the bookies if he did and Josh wanted this as a sort of going away present and it didn't seem to be too much of a serious threat to the natural timeline.

"Peter, you know I seem to do really well at the bookies and am really good at predictions?" asked Josh.

"Yes, you're unbelievably good, you must be psychic! Have you got a prediction?" replied Peter.

"Yes, I believe Liverpool will get to the semi-final of the FA Cup, but get knocked out."

"Who by?" Peter asked.

"Crystal Palace," answered Josh.

"You're crazy! They're rubbish! We've beat them 9-0, there's no way we'll lose to them, no way! I think you are losing your powers!" replied an extremely dubious sounding Peter.

"Oh, it's just a gut feeling, I can just see us losing 4-3. Maybe I am mad, but it's just a weird feeling."

"An insane feeling," insisted Peter. Josh laughed and went along with it. He wasn't going to labour this feeling too much, but it would have been fun to see the look on Peter's face when this came true. Maybe Peter would take a bet on it and make some money, that would be nice and a degree of compensation to be had from such a shock result. Josh said his goodbyes to Peter and left his house for the last time. It was time to go, time to move on to pastures new, to keep away from directly disturbing the natural course of events, at least until March 1st 1990 and the re-appearance of that time bubble. Would Josh enter that bubble again? That was the plan, but would it happen?

Chapter 9

Pastures New

February 1990 was a month of a radical change of environment for Josh; he had indeed very begrudgingly left the Liverpool area for pastures new and hoped to just innocently melt quietly into a new way of living well away from the intolerable pressures of living in his home city. Josh was now living in a beautiful riverside town on the banks of the river Thames; Marlon in Buckinghamshire, a town within a reasonable distance of London but also a town that held a special resonance in Josh's heart since his encounters with his younger dad, Peter Stanton, back in Liverpool.

Marlon had been his dad's childhood home town until his teenage years before he had moved to Liverpool. Josh had known this from his mother Jane when they got to talk about his father in the natural timeline. Josh had got to know his father even better now so where better to spend his last months in the past than the town where his dad grew up as a child, and such a beautiful town it was to be staying in, as long as Josh was continuing to be extremely careful everything should be alright, shouldn't it? Josh really wanted to make the most of his last month in the past before he had to go back to Liverpool and another dreaded date with that time bubble. Josh wasn't looking forward to March 1st 1990 and the discomfort being back in that bubble would mean, but hopefully it would represent closure on this whole adventure and that Josh could resume his natural life back in 2010.

In the meantime, Josh wanted to fully embrace his newly found adopted town. Josh wanted to experience what life was like for his dad growing up here in his younger years. Josh duly immersed himself quietly into local life, being extremely careful not to get involved directly with anything risky or anything that might cause attention. Josh kept himself to himself. He was busy enjoying walking by the river Thames and watching the various boats go through Marlon locks as well as visiting places where his dad would have been present like his old school, childhood home and local park. Josh had really enjoyed this month but it was now the end of February and Josh had to return to Liverpool tomorrow if he was to reacquaint himself with that spherical ball of trouble, that quantum distortion that had given him this adventure. It was time to return to normality, but first Josh thought he deserved to have his last night in Marlon enjoying a little bit of social interaction. Josh really didn't want to be alone on his last night as he felt a significant degree of apprehension at knowing what was to come in Liverpool. He knew the last time he had entered the time bubble he was in a lot of pain so it was definitely not something he was looking forward to at all. Josh noticed there was a quiz night at his newly found local, The Plough on Wycombe Road Marlon, and thought this would be a perfect way to take his mind off tomorrow for at least a couple of hours. This distraction was something Josh really needed, Josh positively thrived in this competitive environment, having decided to join a mature couple who were very happy to have his help, especially as they were up against teams that had at least four members in their team. Josh was naturally competitive, had a good plethora of knowledge especially at sport so he was in his element! Josh was enjoying the company of this mature couple and everything was proving to be a pleasant distraction as the night progressed.

"Thanks for letting me join you!" enthused Josh, "I'm really enjoying this quiz."

"We should be thanking you! We'd have been bottom by miles if you hadn't come to help us," replied this very grateful couple.

"What are your names? I haven't asked you your names," asked Josh.

"We're John and Patricia Chambers, we live just down Wycombe Road, so we're local, are you local?" replied the couple.

"No, I've just been visiting the area. I'm leaving tomorrow but it's been nice to meet you, I'm Josh Stanton, by the way."

"It's a shame you're leaving, you seem a nice lad, we have a daughter the same age as you and wish she would meet someone with your manners, not the undesirables she normally meets."

"Does she come in here at all?" asked Josh.

"Yes, she works here part-time as a barmaid. She's here tonight, behind the bar, she's earning money to help her study, she's really into English Literature and wants to be a teacher or a lecturer one day. She's really clever."

"What's her name?" asked Josh.

"Emma, Emma Chambers. We're so proud of her, she's over there, the girl with dark hair serving that customer," said Mr Chambers. Josh looked around to see and was immediately spellbound at the sight of this very attractive young lady behind the bar; she exuded radiance. She was gorgeous and Josh felt transfixed at her presence. She seemed to light up the room with her engaging smile and demeanour. Josh tried very hard to regain his composure and not betray this mesmerising attraction he was instantly feeling, he didn't want to be seen as unseemly in the presence of her parents and there was a quiz to finish with them. Josh wanted to be a model of decorum and portray the relaxed manner he'd been showing all evening but now it wasn't easy, it wasn't easy at all. Josh's mind was clouded with thinking about this girl behind the bar. He found himself turning round every now and again, all very subtlety and discreetly, just to catch a glimpse of this girl and every time he did it appeared his glimpse was being returned in kind by this vision of beauty. Josh was enthralled but at the same time urgently trying to pull himself together as tomorrow was a very important day. It was soon time to leave but Josh found it very hard to summon the will to actually do it against this attractive pull he was feeling towards this girl, Josh didn't want to leave but leave he must and with a very heavy heart, Josh said goodbye and left.

Chapter 10

Slave to Love

Josh Stanton had endured a terrible night's sleep. It was full anxious thoughts about today's return trip to Liverpool but also frequently punctuated by thoughts of this girl he had seen last night. Josh couldn't seem to get this girl's image out of his head, he was showing signs of being love-struck but it was something he couldn't afford to entertain as he had important business to attend to. Josh duly arrived back in Liverpool and to the area of houses situated behind Liverpool's main stand. Everything proceeded as planned as Josh approached the last boarded up house with the incriminating evidence of the emanating glow of the bubble re-assuring him that normality would hopefully soon be reality, but it was still tinged with a degree of regret, as Josh felt a nagging persistent stream of thoughts about this girl, reluctant to let her go from his mind. It would almost be a relief to get back to 2010 just to be free from the grip of these thoughts, Josh took in a massive inhalation of breath as he proceeded to enter the time bubble, but this time there was something wrong, something very wrong, as Josh made contact with the barrier of the bubble, Josh couldn't pass through the barrier and was repelled back by its discharge resulting in him being thrown back and rendered unconscious. Josh had been knocked clean out.

Josh lay unconscious on the ground for what seemed like an eternity, but was in essence just a few hours but when he came round and began realising where he was and collecting his bearings, to his horror, Josh realised the bubble was no longer present. It had dissipated! Josh was trapped in this period of time, there was no way back! Josh was horror-struck at the predicament, a whole plethora of emotions was going through Josh's mind. 'What an earth am I going to do now? Where am I going to go? What will happen to me?' Josh knew one thing for certain: this was all uncharted territory, but he already realised he couldn't stay in Liverpool a minute longer as there would be a massive danger that he could inadvertently influence the natural course of time in his home city. It was March 1st 1990 and Josh knew he was due to be born on April 10th 1993 and therefore conceived sometime in the summer of 1992, which meant he had only just over 2 years to exist in this period of time. Josh realised from his conversations with Mr Xavier Richardson about the theoretical probability that two Josh Stanton's couldn't exist in the same time concurrently and that one version would simply meld or join with the other, Josh also knew that he was not supposed to be here, it was not in the natural course of the timeline and he was supposed to be born in April, so it was logical to conclude that once his conception had been made this version of Josh Stanton would cease to exist. All this realisation chilled Josh to his very core!

Josh knew that his dad, Peter, and his mother, Jane, were already very close and didn't want to do anything that might even remotely jeopardise that relationship or influence their relationship in any way. Josh Stanton's existence was very much at stake! However, Josh would love to spend more time with his dad it was absolutely essential he didn't and it was a heart breaking necessity to leave Liverpool to make sure Josh didn't weaken in this resolve, but what or where would Josh decide to go next? Josh realised everything now was about damage limitation. Josh wasn't supposed to be here in this time so whatever he did or wherever he went would have some sort of unnatural impact on the timeline, he could only hope it wasn't such a big impact as to cause a 'chip' and therefore once again shatter their natural timeline and alter reality. The logical machinations of Josh's mind were urging him to consider a hermit-like existence somewhere in the very rural countryside, but Josh's mind had the treacherous adversary of his heart urging him to return to Marlon and meet this enchantingly attractive young lady, Emma Chambers, again. Josh was desperately trying to go with his head but the pull of the heart was irresistible, like a moth to a flame, its trance-like stranglehold was too hard to resist. Josh couldn't help himself, he was going to return to Marlon. If Josh had to live 2 years out of time he wanted to have at least a bearable existence and not a lonely one bereft of any comfort. Marlon and hopefully this young lady would be the best hope of providing that, Josh's heart had prevailed against his head! Marlon it was to be for Josh, he sincerely hoped it was the right choice.

Autumn 1990 was now nearing the horizon with indecent haste. Josh had indeed settled in Marlon very well and had fitted in seamlessly into the local way of life. Josh had acted perfectly in an inconspicuous manner and was not drawing undue attention to himself, but there was something fervently challenging him to maintain this situation. Someone called Emma Chambers, who, despite all his best efforts was getting to be more and more the object of his affection. Thoughts of her were becoming all consuming and his heart seemed to yearn more for her as each day passed. Josh was getting to be pretty much The Plough's best customer and Josh had regained a good rapport with her parents. Until now, despite all his inner feelings, he had not initiated anything beyond the polite courtesies with Emma and that was mainly down to feeling inhibited by his feelings for her which had mainly effected his natural exuberance and confident persona but also, Josh realised that given his predicament, it would not be fair in Emma to subject her to a relationship that Josh knew was going to end in a traumatic manner. That was all well and good but Josh's heart wasn't listening to reason and seem determined to gnaw away at him until Josh gave in to his yearning or her.

1st October 1990 was a pivotal evening in changing this status quo. It was quiz night and Josh had again teamed up with Mr and Mrs Chambers and as per usual Josh would exchange longing glances towards Emma which seemed to be reciprocated in kind by her until the glances were exchanged simultaneously in perfect synchronicity. Josh decided this was getting silly and, chastising himself at his inertia, he really had to pluck up the courage to talk to her and tell her how he felt. It was driving Josh mad. Josh readied himself to act but much to his mortification Emma had by now seemed to be engaged in some intense banter by another potential suitor. She was laughing, smiling and joking aplenty, it seemed Josh had missed his chance. He felt his heart sink as he asked Mr Chambers, "Who's that talking with your daughter? Do you know him?" He was trying really hard not to show his chagrin.

"Oh that's Michael, he's her ex-boyfriend, he's just visiting Marlon for the weekend as he's now in the armed forces they still get on very well, but I believe he is getting engaged soon, why do you ask?" asked an inquisitive Mr Chambers, Josh was so relieved his reply was straight to the point.

"I really like your Emma, I've wanted to tell her that for ages," replied Josh his courage now taking over from his timidness.

"Emma likes you as well, she's been asking about you but I think she thought you must be otherwise engaged as you haven't initiated anything that would lead her to think you were interested."

Of course Josh was very interested in Emma, his heart was intoxicated with yearning for her and this was the kick up the backside he needed to finally act, despite his head telling him not to and his conscience being blinded by his feelings for her. What totally mattered was the here and now, the future could be put on hold; a bridge to be crossed at a later date, Josh duly plucked up the courage to ask Emma out and to his delight she enthusiastically accepted.

"I thought you'd never ask! Of course I'll go out with you, you're so cute!" Josh was delightfully elated at her response, but love had made him blind to the dangers. How long could he be happy for?

Chapter 11

The Return to Normality

July 1st 1992.
Josh Stanton and Emma Chambers had now been in a very loving relationship for over eighteen months. Josh was happier than he had ever been in his life and didn't want this utopian era to ever end. Josh was still very much in love but had been ever mindful of trying to create minimal impact by his actions on a future timeline, although he had come by now to be totally absorbed into his present reality so much so that July 1992 had crept up on him like a thief in the night. Being so blissfully happy, Josh still hadn't prepared for what was to come let alone inform Emma about it. Josh hadn't even wanted to contemplate the thought, he would soon no longer be around but now the return to normality was of pressing concern as baby Josh was due to be conceived in Liverpool any day and once that process had been activated, Josh knew he was going to fade from present day existence in this form, leaving Emma totally heartbroken. Josh agonised as to how he could explain it or even if he could afford to explain it to Emma and how implausible and

ridiculous it would seem to her and that she would likely feel very hurt and insulted. Josh couldn't do that to her he had to think very carefully and urgently as how to plan an exit strategy that would cause as little emotional pain as possible. Josh knew he couldn't reveal the truth so had to devise another way.

July 5th 1992 was going to be their final night together. Emma Chambers was blissfully unaware of the bombshell about to be thrust upon her by a totally heartbroken and crestfallen Josh, they had just enjoyed another mutually beautiful day together but Josh had known something Emma had not; it was to be their last together. While Emma was blissfully innocent as time drew near to what Josh had to say to her, he couldn't hide his sadness.

"What's the matter, Josh? You look really sad, haven't you enjoyed today? I have so much. You know you can tell me anything if something is troubling you, as I love you so much," said Emma, sensing the anguish on Josh's face.

"There's something I have to tell you, Emma. You know I love you, but I have to go back to Liverpool tomorrow," replied Josh.

"That's alright, I'll come with you!" enthused Emma.

"I'm sorry but I have to go alone as there's some very personal business I have to attend to." Emma was hurt. Josh didn't want her to come as they had been inseparably close, this was shocking but more was to come when Emma asked about how long Josh would be away. "I think I'm going to be away for a long time, I don't even know if I'm coming back. I'm so sorry, but maybe we should have a time out," said Josh, choking with emotion. Emma was inconsolable.

"You can't mean this, we love each other! I love you so much, how can you just leave me? I thought you loved me. How can you do this to me? You need to explain; you owe me that much, have you got another girl in Liverpool? What is so important that you want to lose everything we've shared together?" said Emma, with ever increasing incredulity, her inconsolable tears being reduced by growing anger. Josh couldn't bear to see how upset Emma was, he couldn't stand the thought of leaving Emma in this state, especially after all they had been through. Josh felt totally responsible and the only respectful course of action was to tell Emma the truth and to hell with the consequences, it was the honourable thing to do, but how would Emma react?

The result was very predictable… very badly! Josh was invited to leave in a very impolite way. This was a truly horrible way to finish what had been the most beautiful time in Josh's existence.

"I can't just leave this era like this," agonised Josh. He knew he had burnt his bridges with Emma for the time being and couldn't bear to think that all the damage was irreparable and that he would fade from existence knowing she hated him. Josh had to do something that might, in time, undo the hurt she was feeling and the answer that came to mind was to leave behind a letter that would explain everything. This last night Josh would pen this very poignant letter to Emma.

"Dear Emma,
I'm so really sorry for all the hurt I've caused you. I loved you so much and being with you was the most beautiful time I will ever experience. I know you think I'm mad and have totally insulted your intelligence but it really is the truth, I would not lie to you. I tried to when I said I was leaving or Liverpool, but I couldn't go through with the pretence as I found it unbearable to mislead you as you mean too much to me. I know you will still not believe what I've told you but it really is the truth. My name really is Josh Stanton, I was born April 10th 1993 and my parents are Peter and Jane Stanton. I was born in Liverpool, I'll live in Liverpool at least until my teenage years when I will go and study at Manchester College. You might want to find me one day to satisfy your curiosity, you will then know all I told you was the truth, however preposterous, so please don't rip this up remember always that I love you so much.

Yours Lovingly,
Josh Stanton, xxxxxx."

Emma Chambers duly received this letter two days later. Emma, still inconsolable and aggrieved was very sorely tempted to rip the whole letter up into a thousand pieces, but against her better judgement refrained from doing so. Somewhere from deeply within there was an intuitive feeling of keeping the letter but storing it safe, fully away out of sight. Emma was still very hurt and angry but to a degree it did feel like a bit of closure. It transpired that fateful letter from Josh was completed and posted just in time, as Josh returned from posting the letter he could feel his life force draining away, all his energy was dissipating and as he looked down at his hands he could sense them fading from view before his very eyes and almost in an instant Josh blacked out of consciousness and ultimately faded totally from this form of existence just as, up in Liverpool, the natural process of Josh's conception had been completed. The return to normality was now here! Or was it?

Chapter 12

Sting in the Tail

December 17th 2009 was approaching; the last few days of term at Manchester College and everything was appearing as it should. A 16 year old, highly promising student, Josh Stanton was where he always destined to be at this time. Josh Stanton's best friend was indeed Ryan Brown, his beloved Liverpool were captained by Stevie Gerrard and had enjoyed that marvellous European Champions trophy in Istanbul. Josh was again popular and there was lots of amiable banter with the Evertonions. Josh lived in Gwladys Street, right behind Everton's football ground, Goodison Park, with his mum, Jane, just as it was always meant to be and unfortunately his dad Peter had been involved in that fatal car accident in 1998 where he lost his life. Manchester United were the massively dominant juggernaut of the premier league under the inspirational guidance of Alex Ferguson, so everything wasn't perfect, but it was normal, it was all the way it should be. Back at Manchester College, Josh was just like any normal sixteen year old lad apart from what seemed like weird vivid dreams every now and then about living in the past and enjoying being in a riverside location in the south. Josh dismissed them as weird and part of his subconscious mind at work, but the dreams and images did seem to be very vivid.

"I've got a very good imagination, maybe I ought to be a writer, not just be into science and physics," nursed a thoughtful Josh. Josh really enjoyed his science work but thought it wasn't unreasonable to explore other diverse possibilities for next term such as English Literature. It might be another string to his bow. Josh duly sought out the opportunity to talk to the English Literature tutor, a certain Miss Emma Chambers. She was 39 years old and had recently moved up north from her childhood place of Marlon! Josh had noticed the mysterious lady several times within college and had developed a compelling curiosity towards her and he'd often notice her looking at him as well, it was like he was divinely drawn to her. Josh was really really nervous as he approached Miss Chambers.

"Hello, Miss Chambers, I was wondering if I could discuss joining an English Literature study group in the future as I feel I could develop talents as a writer," stuttered Josh nervously, feeling very unnerved by his heightened adrenalin levels.

"Of course you can, what is your name?" asked Miss Chambers.

"It's Josh, Josh Stanton," replied Josh. Miss Chambers paused for what seemed like ages before answering.

"That's fine, I'll put your name down, it's really weird but I went out with a Josh Stanton in 1990 and it lasted for 3 years before he disappeared."

"That is weird," agreed Josh.

"The even more incredible thing is that you look just like him! That is so weird!" said Miss Chambers, barely able to conceal her growing fascination with Josh. "I've even kept a letter from him which he wrote to me before he left, I'll have to show it you sometime if the opportunity arises. It's really weird but you really are a dead ringer for him, do you live in Manchester?" asked Miss Chambers.

"No, I come from Liverpool," replied Josh.

"Now this getting really weird! The Josh I knew came from Liverpool, he mentioned it in his letter, he told me some preposterous story that he was born on 10th April 1993 to a Peter and Jane Stanton in Liverpool" said an increasingly anxious Miss Chambers.

"Oh, I was born on 10th April 1993 to Peter and Jane Stanton in Liverpool, this is totally crazy! What on earth is going on?" asked a horrified Josh.

"I do have a confession to tell you, Josh," replied Emma.

"What's that, Miss?" puzzled Josh, sensing even more bewildering confusion to be thrust into his world.

"It's not entirely by accident that I chose to come up to Manchester College to pursue my teaching career, I could have stayed to teach in my native Marlon or I could have chosen to move any number of places, but I chose Manchester and I chose to move here at this period of time," answered Emma.

"But why?" asked Josh, still not grasping what Emma was trying to tell him.

"This letter I have also said that Josh would go on to study at Manchester College if the maths added up and the letter was true in what was being written and that you really were born in April 1993 then it was reasonable to assume that you would be studying at Manchester around this time, I've kept this letter all these years against all my better judgement, but I couldn't ignore my instinctual yearning to find out if the preposterous message could actually have a grain of truth, because if it was I would actually see you again. I can't believe I'm talking to a person that looks exactly the same as I remembered all those years ago, exactly the same, this is so insane! I always thought that in my time here in Manchester I could finally put this matter to rest and move on with my life as I haven't been able to before, as having this letter from my true love, however far-fetched, has really messed with my mind especially as–"

'As what, Miss?' Josh asked, sensing that Emma was troubled.

"Oh, you know meeting other people making new relationships," replied Emma, but Josh could sense that Emma was hiding something from him.

"What is it? Are you alright, Miss?"

"Yes, but this is so unbelievable, I never thought for a minute that this letter would turn out to be true. I would never have…"

“Never what, Miss?” Josh asked Emma, getting evermore concerned at the increasing anguish etched on Emma’s face.

“I’m sorry, Josh, but I need to go now as it is all getting too much for me to take in,” said Emma.

“I couldn’t agree more, Miss,” replied Josh. “It’s too much for me as well but I have got to see this letter that you have for myself, I need to see it as there must be some sort of explanation for all this, as what you are telling me is incredible, but you do seem to have good knowledge about me. I have to find out what’s going on as you’re asking me to believe that I could have been alive in 1992 as a young man when I was born in 1993, it is not humanly possible that this could be right, it is totally absurd! Totally nuts! But when I look at you I do have feelings that we’ve met before. I have incredibly warm and weird feelings when I look at you.”

“Me, too, Josh,” reciprocated Emma.

“I’ll be in touch in the near future and of course you need to see this letter for yourself, I realise that maybe there will be an explanation for all this when you get to see the letter but let’s take a breather for a little while and try and come to terms with what is happening.”

“Yes, Miss, I think that would be wise as this is so intense, but please let me know when I can see this letter,” replied Josh.

Both Josh and Miss Chambers were in full agreement; they were both totally and utterly freaked out by their encounter. Josh was massively dumbstruck at this bolt out of the blue, it was frighteningly chilling and for Miss Emma Chambers it was equally chilling, could this letter she had had in her possession for all these years actually be containing the truth, however absurd? Josh really needed to see this letter for himself so they agreed to meet up at a later date. For the next day or so Josh was walking around in a complete daze, barely able to comprehend the magnitude of it all.

"What on earth is this all about? Surely it must be an incredible coincidence?" What other explanation could it possibly be? During the following days' dinner break, Josh was summoned to Miss Emma Chambers. Josh's heart was racing to almost twice its normal rate as he approached her.

"Here's the letter," said Miss Chambers, handing over a very old looking piece of paper.

"Oh no, that incredible! That is my handwriting how can this be?" shrieked an increasingly hysterical Josh.

"You're not going to believe this but Josh Stanton did tell me something absurd prior to writing this letter, but it was just plain insulting and too stupid for words, so I told him to get lost!"

"What did he tell you?" asked Josh.

"Josh told me that he was from the future, July 2010, and that he had entered into the past through some sort of time bubble and that he had to go back or fade away," replied Miss Chambers.

"Do you know where he had to go? Where was this bubble, as he called it?" urged Josh.

"I believe he wanted to go back to Liverpool and find it somewhere near to Anfield," answered Miss Chambers, now awestruck at her realisation that this indeed was the very same Josh Stanton that she had known as a young lady and somehow his letter had been true all along. This was a person she had been massively in love with and who had left her devastatingly heart broken. Emma showed Josh the letter again and asked Josh to read it.

"Oh my gosh, I was really in love with you." Josh's face was now a brighter shade of crimson at this revelation but he could understand how this could have been a possibility, as there was something magical about Miss Chambers. He could feel a magnetic attraction towards her but now she was a good two decades older that he was, but she was still very beautiful and she still had that indefinable X-factor, something that made the electricity crackle in his heart, but now there was a completely different dynamic to their relationship, how would it develop now?

"What does this make you think, Miss? Or do I call Emma? How are we going to get round this?" wondered Josh.

"I don't know, I really don't know, all this is just unbelievable I don't know what to think. I really need time to get my head around everything," replied a troubled Emma Chambers. Josh and Miss Chambers agreed to take time away from each other to try to come to terms with this massive bombshell thrust upon them. This most definitely was not an easy thing to handle, not easy at all. It seemed that the natural timeline was not totally perfectly reset and that it had deviated, albeit nowhere near as radically as before and the effects don't seem to be too detrimental, but Josh couldn't help thinking that Miss Chambers was holding something back, she did seem very troubled at the end of their last conversation. Josh plucked up the courage to visit Miss Chambers, little knowing that she was going to throw a massive hand grenade into his world.

"How are feeling, Miss?" asked Josh, wanting to keep a respectful manner towards Emma.

"Josh there's something I must tell you, there's something you really need to know," answered a clearly flustered Emma.

"What's that? Are you going to leave? Please don't, I'll go somewhere else if I make you uncomfortable, I can't help what's happening but there is something special about you. I feel it now as I must have felt back then, I'm sorry but I can't help how I feel."

"You're special to me as well, I've thought there was something special about you when I first spotted you but never in my wildest dreams could I ever believe that it was really you, but that's not what I have to tell you."

"What do you need to tell me then?" asked a puzzled Josh.

"I was pregnant! I was expecting our baby! I gave birth to a baby boy but gave him up for adoption. I have to tell you this, I couldn't keep this from you; it's one of the reasons I was so angry with you at the time, I felt I couldn't keep the baby as I wasn't in the right mind. I so regret it but thought it was for the best, you left me totally heartbroken, how could I possibly believe what you had told me? I kept your letter although I don't know why, maybe it was some sort of divine help, but I'm very glad I did."

This was the bombshell to end all bombshells. Josh Stanton was a dad, he had a son out there somewhere, a son who was actually born just before he was born. Where was he? What was he like? How much damage had Josh actually caused to the natural timeline? How would Josh and Emma progress their relationship now? Everything was totally up in the air again! What would happen if Josh never entered the time bubble on 1st July 2010? So many questions, but maybe there was an easy answer to one of them no matter what, Josh and Emma would be together in some manner, Love always finds a way!

The End

EPILOGUE

It was clear that the natural timeline contained a flaw, a chink in the shape of the son born to Josh Stanton & Emma Chambers, as Mr Xavier Richardson so eloquently pointed out just one chink in the windscreen of time could lead to it shattering in due course so it was imperative that their son should be found but where? And even if he was found what could be done as Josh Stanton was a dad & it was his son after all? How would his son prove to have an impact in this imperfect timeline? Josh Stanton was going to find out it was a very big impact indeed, and he was going to find an incredible rollercoaster journey of emotion awaiting him in his relationship with Emma Chambers as the ramifications of his time travelling adventures came back to haunt him.

Josh Stanton was going to find an incredible source of comfort in his most forlorn darkest hour but who was he and why was he so special? What incredible gift was going to help Josh Stanton in his quest to right the wrong of the past & why his mission proves to be so heartbreaking?

Josh Stanton had no choice; he has a debt to pay to mankind & had to success for all our sakes as the very future time was at stake. Josh Stanton was about to undergo another wonderful journey in time! (I hope you will be with him)

If you would like to take the journey with him, please look out for the sequel *Stop Sergio!*